PILATE'S ROSE

Book Six in the *John Pilate Mystery Series*

10th ANNIVERSARY EDITION

Featuring

PILATE'S SHADOW

A New *John Pilate Mystery*

J. ALEXANDER GREENWOOD

PILATE'S ROSE
10th ANNIVERSARY EDITION
Book Six in the *John Pilate Mystery Series*

J. ALEXANDER GREENWOOD

Copyright © 2019 Caroline Street Press

All rights reserved.

ISBN: 978-0-9965229-6-0

Cover designed by Jason McIntyre
TheFarthestReaches.com

Books by J. Alexander Greenwood

Pilate's Cross
Pilate's Cross: The Audiobook
Pilate's Key
Pilate's Ghost
Pilate's Blood
Pilate's 7
Pilate's Rose
Pilate's Shadow

Big Cabin & Dispatches from the West
(with Robert E. Trevathan)

Non-Fiction
Kickstarter Success Secrets
Kickstarter Success Secrets: The Audiobook

Most books available in paperback and ebook formats
wherever books are sold. Visit www.PilatesCross.com
for the latest updates, merchandise and the Clues Blog. Listen to the author
on the Mysterious Goings On podcast. Visit www.MGOPod.com

CONTENTS

CHAPTER ONE
Simon's Pep Talk

At one time, it was terribly amusing, this whole lark of you doing your thing and me chiding you with my clever invective.

I liked it because, as rough as I could be, it was tough love.

You know?

I mean, the harder the truth, the truer the friend that tells it, right?

You put on all the airs and graces of a normal, functional, mature adult--but I see right through all that.

Inside you're as sentimental as James Taylor when the first leaf of fall drops. That's kind of sweet. But...

The sky is changing. Look out that window.

Taters Malley knew they were jerks about ten minutes in. Two financial planners, one in his late forties, the other probably thirty, chartered the *TenFortyEZ*, posing for selfies with smelly cigars, sporting Oakley sunglasses and garish Ed Hardy shirts.

They drank "the good stuff" from a large flask; when that ran out, they helped themselves to Taters' cooler of Modelo, making "beaner" jokes with each fresh bottle.

Taters let that fly, at first, but by hour three, when it was nearing time to head back to the harbor, he was done.

"Guys, time to lock everything down and head back."

The older man shrugged. "Got skunked anyway. Fishing pretty shitty out here, old man," he said, reaching for the cooler. "Guess a little bit of this here burrito juice will help."

The younger man guffawed, swaying on the deck as it rose and fell with the waves.

Taters placed the fishing gear in the locker. "Fellas, can we knock off the beaner jokes?"

"Beaner jokes? What do you mean?" The older man said, sounding genuinely surprised.

"Modelo. It's Mexican beer. And every time you got yourself one you made some kind of Mexican joke."

"Calm down, old-timer," the older man said. "We meant no harm."

Taters felt his blood pressure rise. "Old-timer? You seriously calling me an old-timer?"

The older man shrugged and snorted. "Well, you ain't a spring chicken."

Taters nodded. "Okay."

The younger man looked at the deck a moment.

"Hey Eric, let's chill, okay?"

Eric, the older man, leveled a look at Taters, then nodded.

"Good idea, Donny," he turned and staggered back to the stern, plopping down in a chair, his t-shirt riding up over his belly.

Taters nodded at Donny and finished stowing the gear. Coming back up from the cabin, he caught the pair's discussion.

"The average idiot thinks that's a good idea," Eric said, his lips moving around the stub of his cigar. "Soon as we can get that asshole out of the White House, the sooner we can start making the real money."

"We are losing a ton of fees, that's for fucking sure," Donny said, tipping back his Modelo.

"Typical of his kind. Wants to put the screws to us and give it all away to his people," Eric said, spitting a piece of his cigar overboard.

Taters felt his blood pressure rising again. He thought of Jordan, warning him that his ticker didn't need that kind of crap. He needed to just do his job and keep his mouth shut, especially until he recovered from his upcoming heart surgery.

But Taters wasn't exactly enormous at that sort of thing. He opened the cooler; all twenty-four Modelos were gone. He whirled around, facing the two men who talked shit about his beer as they finished off the last two.

"How much is enough for you guys?" Taters said.

Eric glanced back at him. "What was that?"

"Well, you guys obviously tie down a pretty good living. I don't get a lot of punters on this boat who are on welfare."

"Well," Eric said, taking the stub of cigar from his mouth. "As shitty as the fishing is out here I'm surprised you're not on welfare." He laughed, jammed the cigar back in his maw and raised his hand for a high five from Donny.

Donny smirked, tapped his palm on Eric's, and turned away.

"All kidding aside, Captain," Eric said, turning away and facing the port side of the boat, his eyes seeing, but failing, to comprehend the view. "We're talking financial matters. Regulations and complicated stuff, so— "

"Well, I can only guess you're bitching because your industry is losing about seventeen billion in amped-up fees because of the fiduciary rule."

Eric and Donny looked at Taters, eyebrows raised.

"Well, it's more complicated than that," Eric said, all mirth drained from his eyes.

"I'm sure you think so," Malley said.

"Well, no matter what you may have heard on MSNBC — "

"Son, I was a CPA and a fiduciary for twenty-seven years before I started this charter. I considered it ethical practice and my legal duty to act in the best interests of the beneficiary. I dealt with more than my share of asshole financial advisors ripping off my clients. The fiduciary rule is a good thing, you greedy shit. And by the way, I don't watch MSNBC or anything else. I know how to read. I'm a Republican since before Reagan, back when Republicans worked for the country first, not the party. I'm damn sure not a jerk-off Fox News sheep like you."

Eric stood up unsteadily. "Now just a goddamn minute, mister."

"Sit your ass down," Taters said. "We're going back."

"I want a goddamn refund— "

Taters yelled over his shoulder, "Now who wants welfare? Hold on."

He gunned the engines, pointing the bow towards Key West. Eric fell back in his seat, flipping his middle finger to Taters' back. Donny looked at the boat's wake, rolling his eyes.

Donny and Eric huffed as they jumped from the boat as soon as Taters tied it off to the dock.

"Later, asshole," Eric said.

Cooled off, Taters smiled and waved in acquiescence to Jordan's wishes he work on not being so "excitable," anyway.

He eased his tanned frame from the *TenFortyEZ*, one leg at a time across the two-foot chasm to the dock, grunting with exertion from his aching knee.

"I'm getting too old for this shit," he muttered.

It was late, about seven, and the Key West sun was taking a bow to the delight of tourists across the tiny island. Taters slung his dry bag over his shoulder and headed to his Jeep. Jordan would be home already, as he had radioed in to her that he was on time and could close up shop on his own.

The gravel parking area was dark, the street lights conspicuously asleep. He approached the Jeep, catching movement out of his right eye, heading for him.

He moved sharply to his left, his knee groaning and giving out. "Shit," he moaned.

Rough hands grabbed him by the shoulders and helped him down to his knees.

"Really guys, you're gonna beat me up over the fiduciary rule?"

"Clam up, sir, and come with us quietly," a deep male voice said. This was not Donny or Eric.

"Who the hell are— "

In the ambient light, a handsome man's dark face leaned down into his. "Let's say I'm somebody you don't want to mess with tonight." His words were matter of fact, eyes solemn.

"Okay," Taters said, confused.

The hands on his shoulders all but hauled him to his feet.

"Are you alright, sir?" The black man asked.

"Well, I think my damn knee just gave out."

"Can you walk?" The man said.

"With a goddamn limp," Taters said.

The other man took his dry bag. "Good, because I'm not carrying you, sir," one said from behind Taters.

"What's this about?" Taters said.

"Just get in the car," the black man said.

"Who are you guys?"

The men did not answer. Instead, they walked him to a dark green SUV and helped him in the backseat. The black man sat beside him. "Here," he proffered a blindfold.

"You gotta be shittin' me," Taters said.

The man shook his head slowly.

"Well, damn," Taters said, slipping it over his head around his eyes.

Seated in a small room right out of every cop show interrogation scene, Taters drummed his fingers on a hard metal table, pondering his predicament. Clearly, these were government types. *But why are they after me?* he wondered. He thought back to his last interaction with the feds, struggling to think of what he may have done to earn their ire.

The door opened, and in walked a tall, tanned brunette woman in her early thirties, wearing a United States Navy officer's khaki duty uniform. She held the door for a more mature woman with auburn hair and pale skin, her petite form clad in a tailored black suit. Taters started to stand, but the naval officer gestured for him to remain seated. Her collar insignia denoted the rank of lieutenant commander.

The officer closed the door, and both sat across from Taters, looking him over.

Taters looked back, noting their excellent posture and an unsettling coldness around the eyes. "Umm, howdy. What's up?"

The women exchanged glances.

"Vernon Malley?" she asked.

He nodded. "What's this all about?"

The lieutenant commander's eyes bored into him. "You no doubt recall the events of two years ago, where you and a certain John X. Pilate were involved in a situation related to national security?"

Taters rose up in his chair, pointing at her. "Now wait a minute, we stuck to the deal," he said, his mind wondering what Pilate had gotten him into this time. "We haven't said shit to nobody."

"Did we say you did?" the civilian said.

Taters leaned back in his chair. "Well, no, but you abducted me— "

"Mister Malley, I'm Lieutenant Commander Anderson, and the first thing you need to understand is you were not abducted."

"Well, Lieutenant Commander Anderson, it sure felt like it, what with the manhandling and blindfold, and the cloak and dagger."

She continued, "You were not abducted, sir because none of this happened."

He rolled his eyes. "Oh crap, this again? Look, I didn't do anything wrong. John and I have never breathed a word about that sub— "

"Mister Malley," Anderson continued. "The less you interrupt, the faster this will go."

Taters closed his eyes and took in a deep breath, repeating a stress relief technique Jordan taught him to appease his faltering heart muscle. He placed his weathered hands on the table, palms down, his face striving for impassive.

"Very good," Anderson said. "Now, you recall in our last meeting that if you or Mister Pilate said anything about the submarine or its contents that you would lose everything. Your possessions. Your money. Your freedom."

"Yes." Taters looked from Anderson to the silent civilian, who regarded him with a green-eyed stare.

"Well, we have good news and bad news," Anderson said.

"Which do I get first?"

"The good news," Anderson said. "The good news is you and Mister Pilate probably didn't do anything to violate our agreement."

"Probably?" He said, raising his voice. He caught himself, stopped, took in another deep breath and exhaled. "So, what's the bad news?"

"Someone else did talk, and you're on the hook to help us figure it out."

"Why? You guys clearly have no problems dealing with situations," Taters said, his throat feeling parched. "Does she talk?" He said, gesturing at the other woman.

"Because," the civilian woman said, startling Taters with her first words. "We need to move fast to find out who's talking and why. And that somebody is wary of strangers."

"Well, why don't you just pick that person up lickety-split like you did me," Taters said. "Problem solved."

The civilian woman looked down at the table a moment, then trained her green eyes on his. "Mister Malley, we don't need tactical advice from amateurs."

"Kinda rude," he harrumphed.

She continued. "What we do need is for you to help us get John Pilate to Key West without telling anyone why."

"Why don't you get him here, then?"

"Because that makes things more complicated," she said. "We show up in Iowa—"

"Close enough," Taters said.

"What?" Anderson said.

"Well, he's actually in Nebraska," Taters said. "Jeebus, what kind of spy satellites you guys have, anyway?"

The civilian continued. "We show up in Nebraska, that means we have to involve his family and friends. However, if Mister Pilate gets a call from his best friend who's in a jam, then it's a lot more...tidy."

"Wait just a damn minute," Taters said. "Now look, I'm a patriot, but I have rights here. Like the right not to screw over my best pal just to help you clean up your mess."

Anderson looked at him, impassive. "Two words, Mister Malley. National Security."

"You think you can just— "

"You do this and do it right, and you will never hear from us again," the civilian woman said.

"Oh, pardon my French, but bull fucking shit," he said. "You've already broken your word. Goddamn government."

"Mister Malley, I can only give you my word that we will never trouble you or Mister Pilate again if you assist us," the civilian woman clasped her hands together on the table.

"You Navy, too?"

She only stared back at him.

"NSA? CIA?" he ventured.

She continued to stare.

"Alright." He swallowed dust, looking at the women. "What do I have to do?"

"You just get him here, and then we will connect with you both and tell him what's really going on," the civilian said.

"Which is?"

"Which is that if he doesn't help us figure out who's talking, you and Mr. Pilate are going to be roommates in a black site prison for a very, very long time."

CHAPTER TWO
Iowa...Actually Nebraska

Let's make a list. I'll start. Top three sounds I hate the most:

One: Dr. Sandberg's smarmy social worker on white wine voice;

Two: That idiot at the liquor store in Goss City mispronouncing "Lillet";

Three: The sound of you shaking Wellbutrin XL 600s out of that plastic bottle, twice a day.

Like you're doing right now.

Stop, Dave. My mind is going.

Those pills aren't for me, are they? Especially when you're washing them down with martinis. Is it those men you've killed, John? Drowning out their voices at all? How cliché!

Or is it those you lost? Your grandfather, the failed crime novelist? Sweet old guy. But old. Had to go sometime.

You still miss old Pete Trev then, don't you? Grouchy, cantankerous, one-eyed git. He hated you on sight.

All right, all right...yes, he did warm up to you. Even a broken clock is correct twice a day, you know. Damn that cancer. But you seem to have made up for the loss with that fish-smelling miscreant on the boat. Really, John, a grown man who voluntarily calls himself Taters?

You sure don't medicate over that bitch Samantha. Man, you excused her from class with style, my man, With style. That is one ex-wife that is out of your life.

John, you need to lose ten pounds.

Man, you went through that martini pretty quickly. You're really, really mixing another?

Shit, you cut your finger slicing the lemon. Hurts so good though, that lemon juice in the wound. Don't use Kate's nice tea towel—well, okay, go ahead, then. Fuck it, so now it has a blood stain. You leave blood stains all over the place.

Like the massive stain left by those thugs you and your Hole in the Wall gang blew away outside the jail. The ones even Kate got a shot or two into? So good of Detective Petersen and Commissioner Ryder to sweep all that under the rug.

Just leaves Hilmer Thurman to deal with, huh?

That drink tastes good. The lemon and the Lillet really make that vodka pop.

You gonna kill me now, Snake?

Thurman isn't going to let you get away with it, you know? He will keep on and on. Just like Jack Lindstrom. What a damn psychopath that guy was. Can you believe he chartered a damn plane to come kill you? Guy pulls off the perfect crime—fakes his own death—yet he can't stop picking at that John Pilate scab.

What a dumbass.

"Daddy, where you? Daddy, where you?" Peter giggled, running laps around the base of the oak tree on the edge of the grass, where the cornfields began. His tiny legs pumped in his Baby B'gosh coveralls, hands over his eyes, blond hair waving, cherubic face ecstatic.

Pilate had climbed over his toddler's head, suspending himself in the crook of the oak while Peter played hide and go seek below.

"Find me, Mister!" Pilate said, laughing in spite of himself.

"Where Daddy?" He shrieked, stopping and dramatically uncovering his eyes. "Where Daddy!"

Pilate stifled his giggles as the boy looked all around him, staggering around like toddlers do, not thinking to look up.

Pilate had to go soon, and he was getting his suit dirty wearing it against the rough bark of the tree. He pushed the thought from his mind.

"Where Daddy!" Peter shouted, laughing.

Pilate watched a moment more, as the boy's laughter subsided into concern. "Where Daddy." His voice quieted.

Pilate froze for a moment, feeling a lump in his throat.

"Daddy?" Peter said, the word a lonely accusation, a question and a cry.

"I remember this," Simon said.

"Daddy!" Peter yelled, distress destroying his glee.

"Hey, buddy," Pilate said, quietly.

Peter turned his face upward, his mask of concern shattering into excitement and happiness. "Daddy! Where you hiding!"

Pilate hopped from the tree. "Gonna get you mister!" He chased Peter around as the boy shrieked with delight again. He scooped his son up, caroming him around the yard until they both fell in a heap of tickles and laughter.

"I love you, sweet boy," Pilate said, nuzzling his neck.

"Daddy," Peter said, hugging Pilate's neck.

"John?" Kate called from the backdoor. "Better get going."

Pilate inhaled his toddler's scent, picking him up and carrying him to inside. "Let's go, mister, we have places to be."

A dispassionate, albeit threatening camera stared Pilate in his face like a low-rent HAL from *2001: A Space Odyssey*. He squirmed at the head of a long conference table in the bland Lincoln, Nebraska office of the opposition's counsel, Edward Mann.

A gaunt stenographer prepared to record every word of the proceedings, clacking on her stenotype as the attorneys on both sides of the table shuffled papers, passed notes and looked bored waiting for Mann to switch the camera on.

"Stop Dave," Simon said.

Dryly referred to by John's attorney Magnus Peck as a "sore neck lawyer," Mann was a rare winner of the genetic lottery; Pilate couldn't tell if he was thirty-five or fifty. The guy was handsome, his face mature but almost completely unlined, his head of hair full, with nary a fleck of gray.

"He's had a lift," Simon snickered. *"Or at least a lotta facials. Maybe he owns stock in Just For Men."*

Pilate's mind drifted back to the events that led him to this moment. Frechette was Pilate's publishing agent, and he had absconded with more than six hundred thousand dollars' worth of proceeds from his bestselling book about his brush with murder in Cross Township. He had also taken a few bucks from a couple of other clients, but Pilate held the lion's share of loss.

Frechette had been on the run more than a year, haunting the Caribbean and eventually Central America, blowing stolen cash on booze, young men, and fine living. He slipped up when his mother took ill, and Frechette brazenly—or stupidly—returned to New York to be at her side.

His mother's illness was an FBI ruse: they posted fake news stories about how Mrs. Frechette wanted to see her son one last time before she passed. When he arrived at the nursing home, his mother, in fine health, was indeed glad to see him, as were two FBI agents.

So began the criminal proceedings, which upon sentencing will likely give Frechette a few years in the pokey.

But there was still the matter of Pilate's money. Frechette claimed he spent it all. Pilate sued him, and reluctantly gave interviews to the media—a few of them angry, sarcastic and fueled by vodka.

Frechette countersued Pilate. For libel.

Mann stood, switched on the camera and stated the time. "We're going on the record and we'll try and turn the video recorder off any time we take a break. If you would like to administer the oath, we'll get started."

Pilate swore to tell the truth. That out of the way, Mann proceeded.

"If you could sir, start out and give us your name."

"John Xander Pilate."

"Thank you, Mr. Pilate. Now, as it relates to your ability to give testimony today, do you know of anything, medical condition or otherwise that will interfere with your ability to understand the questions that I'm asking you and to give us complete and truthful answers?"

"No."

"For instance, you don't have any medical condition where you're on some kind of prescriptive drug?"

"I am on prescription drugs, not of such that it would affect my mental capacity."

"Do you see a psychiatrist?"

"Object. Not pertinent," Peck said.

"What if I do? Why is that any of your business?" Pilate asked, his voice rising.

"Mr. Peck, it is pertinent," Mann said, his voice calm. "Now will you advise your client to answer my questions and cooperate?"

Peck nodded. "John, answer the question."

Pilate glanced sideways at his attorney, then back to Mann. "Yes, I do from time to time. I also take antidepressants and a statin drug for high cholesterol. My junk still works on the rare occasion I get to use it, so I don't take any blue pills yet. Satisfied?"

"Why do you see the psychiatrist?" Mann said, his face betraying a faint smirk.

"What?"

"For what reason? What is your diagnosis?"

"I'm not answering that," Pilate said.

"You're under oath."

"Tough," Pilate looked at Peck, keening for a lifeline.

"Eddie," Peck said. "I'll object to the scope of the notice. My client is not under a doctor's care for any condition that would affect his judgment or this testimony. I somewhat doubt he would be in a position of leadership in law enforcement if he were. So, if you are trying to go down the road that he is mentally unstable, we'll stop this deposition right here and now and go call the judge."

"Really, Magnus?" Mann said, smirking. "Subparagraph two asks—"

"Which is different from your question, which was related to the purpose of this deposition."

"Don't lecture me, Magnus. I can just keep asking until you answer me," Mann said, a smile creeping across his face as he leaned back in his chair.

"Try me," Peck said, folding his arms in front of him on the table.

Mann smiled.

"Okay, Mr. Pilate, by whom are you currently employed?"

"I'm self-employed," Pilate said.

"And previously?" Mann said, looking at a yellow legal pad.

"Previous to?"

"Previous to being self-employed."

Pilate sighed. "I was the constable of Cross Township."

"And where is that?"

"Where?"

"Cross Township," Mann smirked again, favoring Pilate with his charming, boyish countenance. "Oh yes, the quaint southeast corner of our fine state."

"If he weren't such an asshole he could be likable," Simon whispered.

"Nebraska," Pilate said.

"Thank you. This will move more quickly for you if we can just stick to the facts."

"Happy to," Pilate said. "If you do the same."

"So, constable. That a law enforcement position?" He rubbed his chin.

"Yes, though not really a police officer. More of an armed code enforcement deputy."

"Armed?"

"Yes."

"Yes, well, the world knows full well about your adventures with firearms."

"Object to—" Peck started.

"What's that supposed to mean?"

Mann shrugged. "Just that it is well documented you have been involved in numerous violent incidents."

"Law enforcement often involves violence," Pilate said.

"Oh, I know," Mann said, leaning back in his chair. "I was talking about before your term as an armed code enforcer."

Peck started to speak again.

"Before?" Pilate said.

Mann nodded. "Yes. Before that."

"Oh, so before I saved twenty kids in a classroom of students being held hostage without firing a shot?"

"Let's move along," Mann said, leaning forward again, slipping on his glasses and perusing a legal pad.

"Nice job, John. If not a little vainglorious," Simon said.

"Mr. Pilate, why were you fired as constable of Cross Township?" Mann said, dispassionately, his eyes regarding Pilate.

"Object to the form. Argumentative," Peck said, his voice dry and detached.

"Answer the question, please," Mann said.

"I was not fired as constable. I resigned."

"Why? Or is fired just a writer's term for resigned under duress?"

"Object to the form. Argumentative. This has nothing to do with—" Peck started.

"I am establishing the financial and professional status of Mr. Pilate," Mann said, his eyes remaining on Pilate.

Pilate looked at Peck, who wordlessly looked down to his legal pad.

"Mr. Pilate?"

"Yes?"

"Answer the question?" Mann said, eyes migrating to his notes.

"Could you repeat the question? I'm confused."

"You're playing with him, John," Simon said. *"You already know this is going to bite you in the ass. Same old, same old."*

"Why did you resign your job?" Mann said, icy. "Was it because you no longer needed the money or because you had just presided over the murder of more than a dozen people?"

"Object to the form, argumentative," Peck said. "Has nothing to do with—"

"Magnus, this is my deposition," Mann said. "I'll thank you for letting me conduct it." He turned from Peck to Pilate. "Now do you understand the question? Do you understand the word fired or is that not in your highfalutin college professor vocabulary?"

"I don't know. I understand it in general but perhaps not in your context. Guess I'm not up on my sore neck lawyer vocab," Pilate shot back.

Peck whistled silently to himself.

Mann's face reddened.

"Okay, well if there's anything else here, any other terms I use that confuse you, just make sure you point that out to me and we can try and avoid that, okay?" His tone cooled. "I understand that in certain states of mind it's easy to get confused."

"What the hell does that mean?" Pilate demanded.

Mann smiled. "Well, if you are under a psychiatrist's care, for example, you might get confused. Medication tends to make some people foggy."

"Object—" Peck said, his lawyerly dispassion evaporating.

"Just ask your damn questions," Pilate said, his eyes looking into the camera lens.

"Open the pod bay doors, HAL," Simon said.

"Do I need to repeat the original question?"

Pilate inhaled and did his best not to look rattled. He breathed out. "I resigned because I had no desire to continue a career in law enforcement. I only took the job because your client robbed me blind to fund his trips to an assortment of resort hotels that cater to his flamboyant lifestyle."

Pilate flicked his eyes to Frechette, who looked away with a dramatic flip of his head to the right.

"If you were, quote, robbed blind, unquote, then how could you leave a job? How are you supporting yourself and your family?" Mann said.

"My wife works," Pilate said.

"I see," Mann said. "So, she is head of household?"

"What?" Pilate said.

Mann looked up at Pilate over his reading glasses. "For tax purposes?"

"Give me a break."

"But you freely admit that you have a contract with Mr. Frechette, do you not?" Mann said, looking down his nose through reading glasses at Pilate.

"That's not in question," Pilate said.

Without looking up, Mann stated, "Please advise the witness to respond to the question. We need a simple yes or no."

Peck cleaned the frames of his glasses with the pointy end of a folded Post-It Note. "Noted," he said, not looking away from his spectacles.

"Yes, I had a contract with the embezzler in question," Pilate said.

Mann sighed.

"You know, Mr. Pilate, some folks think you're some kind of hero, but I don't. My client doesn't. They just see that you had a contract with him, wherein he is allowed to share in the profits of the book that he helped publish, you sued him, slandered him and are using your fifteen minutes of fame to try to destroy his character. Character assassination, just the way you assassinated those people—"

"Object to form," Pilate's attorney said. "You want to ask questions or grandstand, Eddie? We can end this right now if you want to abuse my client."

"Don't tell me how to handle my deposition, Magnus," Mann said, his voice rose. "This is my deposition, and I will ask the questions here."

"You have ways of making me talk, eh?" Pilate affected a bad German accent.

Peck shot him a look that said, *"Shut the hell up, John."*

Mann's face darkened. Pilate looked past him to Frechette, who, despite the tan he cultivated while on the run in Central America managed to look ashen.

"Mr. Pilate, I can stop now, call the judge and explain to her that you are purposely obstructing these proceedings."

"What will happen then? Will she fine me for contempt? Maybe take all my money? Too late for that. Your client did that when he stole all the profits from my book."

"Okay, everyone, let's just—" Peck said.

Pilate felt his cell phone vibrating in his pocket. The deposition grilling had made him sweaty and sticky in his suit; his hand moistened just reaching into his breast pocket to stop the notification.

"You need to take that?" Mann said, raising an eyebrow above a red rope binder.

"No, it can wait," Pilate said. "Probably nothing important, except maybe my kids or wife calling."

"Oh yes, well maybe you should take it, considering."

"Considering what?" Pilate said, a tremor in his voice.

Mann shrugged, dropping a notepad on the conference table. "Just that your... um, lifestyle seems to put your family in danger quite a bit, leaving them to fend for themselves," his voice dropped to a whisper. "Some might say that's kinda cowardly."

"You son of a bitch," Pilate said, lunging at Mann.

"John, no!" Peck yelled, reaching for him, knocking over a bottle of water and dousing his notes.

Mann held his hands in front of his chest, palms facing a red-faced, snarling Pilate, who stopped an inch from Mann's face.

Pilate backed off and sat down slowly in his chair, loosening his collar.

"We need a break, here," Peck said, his voice rattling.

Mann smiled, smoothed his tie and leaned over the recorder. "We are off the record. It's three p.m." He turned it off and followed the stenographer out of the room, Frechette in tow.

Peck cleaned his glasses and remained silent.

"I'm not sorry."

"John, this isn't about being sorry. It's about that gimcrack ambulance chaser getting you all wrapped around your own axle to get what he wants for Buddy Boy."

"Fuck that," Pilate said, reaching for a bottle of water.

"John, this is stressful, I know," he said.

"No, it's a pain in the ass. You know what's truly stressful? Nearly getting your ass shot off. Having people come after your family," Pilate said. "Losing your family," he added, his voice breaking.

"John, you're all in. You need to chill out for a bit. Let me get a continuance on this—"

The door to the conference room swung open, with Mann, Frechette, and the stenographer theatrically striding to their seats.

Mann leaned over to the camera, turned it on and said, "It's three-thirteen p.m., we are off the record." He turned it off, wordlessly packing his red ropes, legal pads, and the camera into bags.

"We done?" Peck said, failing to conceal the surprise in his voice.

"For now," Mann said, cool and emotionless.

Pilate stood up quickly. Mann didn't flinch, though Frechette started and gasped.

"We'll be in touch," Mann said, making eye contact with Pilate and Peck, smiling as he walked out.

"What the fuck was that?" Peck said. "He ended the deposition with pages of questions on the table."

"Is that unusual?"

"You bet your ass."

"Does that mean we're done?"

Peck shook his head. "No, probably he's just done for today. And unfortunately, we now have video of you losing your mind he can show the judge or maybe a jury down the road. Sorry pal, not your best moment."

"Freaking great." Pilate whipped off his sweaty suit jacket and dropped it on the table. It made a clunk sound as it hit the table, reminding Pilate that his phone had rung earlier. He fished it out and read "Missed Call: Taters Malley."

"Him again?" Simon said.

CHAPTER THREE
Iowa…Actually Nebraska

Are you really going back outside to that ridiculous door bar of yours? Who makes an old front door into a backyard bar?

Oh yeah. John Pilate.

Clouds are pretty dark. Could be showers.

So, where were we? Oh yes, Kate took the kids to see Grif at the assisted living center. You're batchin' for a few hours and decide to make a shaker or two of martinis. My lord, man, you've been out here five minutes and another one is already down your gullet.

Lighten up, Francis.

What is that? Sprinkles? Rain? Better go inside. Look at the thunderheads. Good, let's go inside. Wait, what are you doing with your keys to that Dodge Ram Commissioner Ryder loaned you? Playing constable again?

That was thunder, John. And you have no business driving after downing two very large martinis, even in this one-horse town.

I'm afraid, Dave.

The first drink was hail fellow well met; the drink that set things right. That drink was charming and funny and full of hope. The sun was barely thinking of setting on that first drink. It made short work of the pain in his side, aching where he was once peppered with buckshot. It was like the first two strokes inside a warm woman; feels incredible and there are still good things to come. He swirled the last swallow of his drink around in the Nick and Nora-style martini glass, an unwelcome wave of despondence washing over him. If he were honest with himself, Pilate would acknowledge that some nights the last drink became two, then three.

Pilate wasn't drunk, per se, but sure as hell wasn't sober as a judge. He wavered a little, leaning over the lantern hissing and aglow atop the old oak front door, which lay horizontally before him, part of his makeshift outdoor speakeasy. He had christened it the Frontdoor Backyard Bar last year and it had served him well until this fall.

The fall powered up the ugly lights that said *go home*; exposing the wood that curled from exposure to sun, snow, and rain. Pilate's well-intentioned, cheap blue hardware store tarps had done little good in preserving it. Slivers of veneer and splinters fell off every time he touched it. He was at pains to figure out how to save the ridiculous horizontal prop for his teetering body.

"What's with you, man?" Simon asked.

I don't know. I just don't want it.

"Want what?" his inner voice pressed.

Anything. I just want...I just want everything to slow down.

"I think you just want to hide," Simon said. *"Mind if I smoke?"*

Hide from what?

"Yourself. You never think you're good enough, and I think you want to mess up anything and anyone who does. Poor Kate. Poor kids."

Pilate tensed. *Shut up, would you? I—*

He felt his phone vibrating in his pocket. He looked at the screen and smiled, but it reminded him that he hadn't returned Taters' call earlier this afternoon.

"Well, well if it isn't the best boat captain in all the—"

"John?" Taters said, cutting him off.

"Hey man, how you doing?" Pilate said, watching the sun disappear over the barren cornfields to his west.

"Well, I been better, my seafaring pal," Taters said, clearing his throat.

Pilate blinked. *Seafaring.* The code word when things were going to shit.

"Your ticker?"

Taters paused a moment. "Yeah. My ticker. Got some flutters, and more than the usual ones when I see a nice bikini."

"What's going to happen? More surgery?"

"Maybe. Hey, look, Jordan's on her way home and I can't talk long. I don't want to worry her, but I'm a little... well, you know."

Taters and John never thought they would actually engage in this type of spycraft, but the code word idea seemed like a good idea after their past interactions with the government. Taters, ever the honest man, was having a tough time keeping up the pretense and was trying to end the call quickly before electronic eavesdroppers caught on.

"When do you want me there?" Pilate asked his friend, pushing his full glass away on the peeling bar.

"Soon as you can," Taters said. "We may schedule the procedure for later this week. It could be nothing, but—"

"Say no more," Pilate said. "I'll book a flight."

"Okay. Call me when you get it worked out. Bringing the family?"

"Wish I could, but Kara has school, and Kate has to teach, and Pete, well Pete has to be Pete with his mama and sis."

"That's probably best," Taters said. "I'd appreciate it if you didn't worry them at all. You know? Just tell them it's something else."

"Understood."

"Either way, I gotta go. Call me when you get arrangements made?"

"You bet, pal. And don't worry, everything's gonna be all right."

"I admire your optimism," Taters said, ending the call.

"Shit," Pilate said. He looked at the fading sunset. "Damn damn."

"Well, well well," Simon said. *"Looks like Uncle Sam has plans for you."*

Great.

Now he had to explain to Kate why he had to go to Key West—and it couldn't be the truth.

"It's for her protection," Simon said. *"Think of the kids."*

I'll tell her tomorrow.

"Coward."

Shit. He stretched, unsteady and stiff, feeling his back muscles protest.

He snatched up the lantern and swayed like John Wayne walking the streets of Rio Bravo as he crossed the thirty yards of backyard to the kitchen screen door.

"Now where were we before your buddy the sea dog interrupted us?" Simon asked, exhaling mental cigarette smoke.

Shut up.

He estimated it had to be nearly ten-thirty, but the light was still on in the living room. The kids were always in bed by eight, no matter their protestations, so he assumed Kate must have fallen asleep on the couch, her face bathed in the light of the corn stove.

He walked gingerly into the kitchen, setting the vanquished lantern and his empty glass on the counter, inhaling deep and steadying himself.

Guess I'm telling her tonight. I should drink some water.

He turned to the faucet, filled a cup and downed it. A couple of aspirin might be a good idea, too, but that could wait. No need to rattle that bottle and wake that rebuke tonight. He inhaled deeply again and walked as steadily as he could into the living room.

He was surprised Kate wasn't asleep on the couch. Instead, she sat upright, her face cool and immobile as the statue in the quad. Oddly, sitting beside her was Cusack, their Irish friend who owned the local bed and breakfast.

"What is this, an intervention?" Pilate said, forcing a snort.

"Sure as fuck is," a man's voice said from the shadows of the staircase.

Pilate squinted at the shadow. "Who the hell are you?"

"I'm sorry, John," Cusack said. "He made me bring 'im here."

"Shut up, you Mick fuck," the man said, punctuated with the unmistakable sound of a shell shucking into a shotgun chamber.

Pilate slowly raised his hands, noticeably trembling. "N-now, just a minute, friend—"

"I ain't your friend, and you best understand your bitch and buddy here have about a minute to live. Less if you move."

"Leave them out of it."

"Like you did my brother?"

"Brother?"

"He was one of the guys you three turned into a pile of dog food outside the jail last year."

Kate winced, her eyes shone watery panic in the dim light of the room.

"Yeah, bitch. I know what you did last summer, or whatever," the man chuckled mirthlessly. "Momma said they had to have a closed coffin. Face looked like a fucking plate of Hamburger Helper."

"Look, your brother, whoever he is…was part of a mob trying to kill us—" Kate said.

"Shut up, bitch. I woulda been here sooner, but I just got out," he contorted his face strangely, "and I am here to chew bubble gum and kill people. I will add that I am fresh out of bubble gum." He laughed at his poorly cribbed joke, which he had evidently rehearsed.

Pilate could tell he wasn't half as badass as he acted.

"He's scared. Determined, but scared, John," Simon said.

Pilate's mind raced back to another call he forgot to return. *So that's why Morgan Scovill called me from prison the other day. To warn me.* Pilate silently cursed himself for forgetting to follow up on the call—too preoccupied with that asshole Mann's deposition.

He sized up his options. At this range, the shotgun would obliterate Kate and Cusack with one shot before Pilate could cover two steps.

"Even if you were sober as a judge," said Simon, Pilate's interior friend and tormenter. *"Which you most certainly are not."*

Pilate tensed up, his eyes darting to Kate's, her eyes red and frantic. She silently implored him to do something, anything, to protect their children sleeping upstairs.

Got no choice but to rush the guy and take the blast.

"So, Mister Bookwriter, why don't we get this over with. Have a seat there with your pretty wife and buddy and we'll end all our problems."

"Can't we talk about this?"

"We just did," the man stepped out of the shadows. In the soft light of the living room, he was thin, gangly and ugly.

The foul air of a meth veteran hung about him. He wore the hideous badge of poorly inked prison neck tattoos under an old jean jacket. He looked like a zombie version of Reverend Jim from that old TV show *Taxi.*

"It's meth head Reverend Jim," Simon whispered.

Meth head Reverend Jim's hands were unsteady holding Kate's twelve gauge, his finger caressing the trigger.

"Who was your brother?" Pilate said.

His head jerked up at Pilate. "Huh?"

"Your brother. Who was he? His name?"

"You didn't know him. You just killed him," he said, his lips curling back to reveal yellow stumps of ruined teeth. "He was just tryin' to provide for his family. Now quit stalling and git your ass on that sofa." He gestured with the shotgun barrel.

"Alright," Pilate said. "Just take it easy."

"John," Kate said, her voice trembling.

"Do not mention the kids upstairs," Simon hissed in Pilate's brain. *"If he doesn't know about them, he won't hurt them."*

Simon, he knows we have kids. What's to stop him from going upstairs after he blows us all away? He's going to kill us all.

"Shit."

As if on cue, a child's voice carried down from the top of the stairs. "Daddy? Mommy? What's going—"

Jim looked up, swinging the shotgun towards Kara's voice. Unsteady, Pilate leaped across the room, desperate to intercept the man before he got a bead on his daughter.

"Run, Kara!" Kate screamed, launching herself from the sofa.

Pilate came within two feet of the man, who cursed and swung back, facing the now-standing Kate and Cusack. He missed.

Pilate landed at the foot of the stairs, hitting his head, hard. He rolled over, trying to rise to his feet. Glass from the picture window behind Kate and Cusack shattered revealing the unmistakable, rangy shape of Jeremy Ryder after he fired one shot through it.

Pilate glimpsed Ryder's angular face bathed in the porch light, one eye squinting from behind his smoking six-shooter.

The wind rushed out of Pilate as the body of the meth head collapsed atop him. Blackness overtook Pilate, the collective shrieks of the farmhouse fading with his vision.

"John," a laconic drawl of familiarity awakened him. "John, you all right?"

Pilate opened his eyes. "Kate! Kara—"

"They're fine."

"Pete?" Pilate tried to stand up, though he was woozy as hell. "Gotta stop that guy—"

"John, listen to me," hands grasped his shoulders and shook him, "Look at me. John, look at me. It's Ryder. Everyone's okay."

Pilate fixed his vision on flinty grey eyes.

"Hey, it's Robocop Cowboy," Simon said.

"Aye, John, we're all grand," Cusack said from over County Commissioner Ryder's shoulder. "Kate's outside on the porch with the kids."

"We called EMS," Ryder said, his eyes flicking to the body covered by Kate's afghan on the floor. "Well, the meat wagon, in this case."

"What happened?"

"I was on the porch for the last couple minutes of your discussion with that piece of shit," Ryder shrugged, dabbing at a bloodstain on his ostrich boot with his handkerchief and some spit. "When your daughter distracted him and you took that clumsy dive, I put a .44 slug in his left eye socket. Tough shot, too, what with Kate trying to hop up and kick his ass."

"Oh," Pilate said.

"Sorry for the mess," Ryder said, his eyes sidelong at the blood splatter. He gestured at Pilate. "I think you're gonna want to burn that shirt. And your rug. And maybe repaint the whole room," he said, looking around them.

"Or just move," Pilate said, sitting up with a groan. "How did you know?"

"Got a call from a CI," he said, looking back at Pilate.

Pilate stared at him uncomprehendingly, his hand tenderly touching his temple.

"Confidential Informant. Told me this shitbird was getting out and wanted some payback from you, me, your wife and our Celtic friend here. Think he was saving me for last."

"Morgan Scovill. He called."

Ryder nodded, clicking his tongue. "We might need to speak on his behalf at the next parole hearing."

"Yeah. Definitely," Pilate sighed. "I gotta see my family."

"They're right outside. You need to get looked at when EMS gets here," Ryder said, a siren wailing in the distance. "Won't be long now."

Pilate nodded. "Thanks."

"No charge." Ryder made a face and looked at his boots. "Though these boots ain't cheap. Gonna be a bitch if I can't get the blood out."

"Young Peter is asking 'where Daddy.' And you're all staying at my place tonight," Cusack said, leaning in. "I have a cask of something good for us waiting. I think we need a wee dram."

"Or two," Pilate said.

"Feck it. Ten."

CHAPTER FOUR
House and Home

Well, alrighty then. I'm apparently along for the ride. Can you see me in the rearview mirror? No? Just your buckshot-scarred face. You used to be able to see me in the mirror. Right behind you.

Welcome to the Cross Township Casual Horrors Ride. Please, only three people per Doom Buggy, thank you. No flash photography if you know what's good for you.

"He needs me, Kate," Pilate said.

"Really? And we don't? You do recall there's a criminal's brains all over the living room, right? We were all nearly killed last night."

"Well, can't you stay with Cusack while I'm gone? Just a couple of days?"

"John, Taters will understand. If he finds out you left us to come see him in the hospital after all this, he'll never forgive you." Kate wiped down the kitchen counter, her eyes avoiding his.

"Kate," Pilate took her by the shoulders. "Please look at me. Ryder will keep a security detail on you at Cusack's. There's not going to be a problem."

"John, that's the thing. There's always a problem, isn't there?"

"What the hell does that mean?" He released her.

"You're just running away," she said. "There's a problem here and—"

"That guy is dead," he said. "There is no reason to believe there's more to come. You're safe."

"I wasn't talking about another killer looking for retribution or whatever," she said.

"You've been trying to leave Cross since the day you got here." She turned away from him and sprayed Windex on the counter. She started working on a stain with a sponge.

"Yes. Yes, I have. And if it weren't for you and the kids —"

"Oh, don't you dare put this on us," she said, turning back to him.

"Fine. Fuck it. But I can't stay here anymore. Not now. I've got a friend in trouble and you're giving me a guilt trip? Besides, you know it's best I get away from you all. You'll be safer. You think that guy with the shotgun was bad? Hilmer Thurman is still on the loose, and he'll want payback for what I did as constable just as bad. Sooner or later. I'll just get you guys hurt if I stay."

"What? Are you hearing what you're spewing? You just said we were safe if you leave because there's nobody left to hurt us, and now you're saying we're not safe?"

Pilate felt the rage circulating through his body. "You're not listening, Kate. You know what I mean. I love you guys."

"You keep telling yourself that," she said. "You selfish shit. You want out? Do you want to get away from us? You want to be single again? Then go. Get the fuck out. But don't tell me you're trying to save our lives, or see your sick friend, or some such bullshit." Her face reddened, defiant eyes glistening with tears.

"Kate, you know, all I have brought you is—"

She wiped her eyes with a fist. "You brought me such joy. We were happy. Now all you do is mope around and act miserable. So go. You get a pass. Go to Key West. I'll clean up the mess here," she knocked the Windex bottle into the sink. "Go do whatever you need to do to get your shit together."

"Look, your majesty, I don't need your fucking permission," he said.

"No, but you apparently need something I can't give you."

He reached for her. She pulled away. "Pack your shit, John. Tell the kids you have to go work on your book or see Taters. Tell them you'll be back if that's the truth."

"Don't say that. I love the kids. Peter and Kara are my kids."

"No, John. They're ours. And they will miss you," Kate said, biting her lip and hugging herself.

"Will you?" Pilate asked, his voice wavering.

"So, you going or what?" she asked, looking at the floor beneath her boots.

"Yes."

"Then do it, before the kids get home," she made a beeline for the living room, calling over her shoulder, "Go, you selfish bastard. Just go."

CHAPTER FIVE
Hello Old Friend

On your right you will see the homes of some of Cross Township's leading citizens, including Mrs. Drum, whose lawn apparently attracts people with the urge to defecate.

Speaking of defecation, the clinically insane failure of a human being that is Harley Cordwainer, aka King Shit, is on his front porch right now, clad only in a bathrobe and fuzzy slippers. He's apparently cursing the thunderheads. Well, we're in for a treat, folks, as he just flipped us the bird. Cordwainer's bird! Wave back, everyone!

On your left you will see the gothic silhouette of Cross College, complete with library clock and bell tower, admin building, gym, cafeteria, classrooms and other places where middling academic careers go to die.

Just right of that is the president's residence, still reeking of the stink of murder and criminality that was Jack Lindstrom. There's faculty housing right over there, where our own John Pilate shagged Kate Nathaniel into submission, then served her a grilled cheese with Miracle Whip. Classy.

Pilate deplaned at Key West International, the sticky, warm sea air tripping olfactory triggers, taking him back to his love for the salty, seedy seduction of island life. Waiting to pick up his bag, Pilate felt his cellphone vibrate in the hip pocket of his Levis.

It was a notification of voice mail. Pilate pressed the phone to his ear and listened.

"Hey, it's a voice from your past. I could use a friend right about now if you have some time. Call me?"

Kay. Kay Righetti.

"Oh, crap," Simon said.

Two years already. A couple of bad guys had tossed Trevathan's place and Kay was the police officer who took his report. Lovers almost immediately, Kay had helped Pilate with a nasty Bahamian drug ring. For her trouble, she nearly took a bullet and ended up leaving the force—and Key West. He never expected to hear Kay's voice again. There were so many unexpected things these days.

He swallowed hard and hit the "call back" button.

Three rings and then, "Hi."

"Live, not Memorex," Simon blurted.

John felt a rush of blood to his cheeks. "Hi."

Her voice was as confident as he remembered. Once a cop, always a cop—they instill a sense of authority whether intentional or not. "Word on the street is you're back in Key West every now and then, writing books and hanging out with your captain buddy."

"The word is correct," Pilate said. "I have no street words about you, though. What brings you back?"

"Oh," she cleared her throat. "A little matter with my condo. I never actually sold it. Was renting it to a dude who trashed it, so I'm down here cleaning up and getting it ready to sell. That and a few other loose ends."

"I see," he said.

She was silent a moment.

"Kay? You alright?"

"Mostly," she said. "I just…"

"What?" He said, stepping away from a portly man trying to reach past him to collect a suitcase off the baggage return.

"Well, I just wish I could see you. Wish you were here in Key West so we could talk about some stuff."

"You want to get dinner?" he said. "Tonight?"

"When can you book a flight? That would be great," she said, laughing.

"Great? What would be really, really great is you not telling your ex-lover that you're in town," Simon interjected. *"Especially at this very moment when Taters needs you."*

"No need to," Pilate said. "I'm in Key West right now."

"Get out," she shouted.

"No, seriously," Pilate said. "I'm hailing a cab right after I get my bag."

"Holy shit," Kay said. "You want to meet me at the Green Parrot?"

"Just say when."

"An hour?"

"John. What the hell are you thinking?" Simon said, his voice growing fainter.

"See you there," Pilate said.

"Excellent. I can't believe it. So glad," Kay sounded relieved and excited all at once. "You can tell me about your wife and kids," she said. "Green Parrot, seven o'clock." She ended the call.

"Well, I guess that comment makes it pretty clear. There's not going to be any sexy time tonight," Simon said. *"That's a good thing, buddy! You have my blessing now."*

Pilate waved a cab down and the driver to drop him at Trevathan's place.

He called Taters. No answer.

Must be out on the boat.

"Hey man, it's me. Flight got in ahead of time. Tailwind. You'll never believe who called me while I was midair. Kay. She's back in town. I'm going to meet her for a quick drink or two and then I'll head your way. We gotta figure all this stuff out." He ended the call, looking out the window as the tourist Mecca that is Duvall Street rolled into view.

Pilate had just enough time to drop his bags, plug in his cell phone to the charger and check out Trevathan's place to ensure it hadn't had any unwanted leaks, visitors or critters in the months since he was last there.

Seeing no problem, he took a quick shower and changed into a black V-neck t-shirt. His workouts at the college gym and running the hills back in Cross had helped him tone up, though he figured the massive consumption of potato juice was holding him back from getting as svelte as he wanted.

"You look fine, man," Simon said. *"Hey, you're in your forties and still have good hair. That alone is an achievement."*

Pilate brushed his teeth, ran a hand through his good hair and scooped up his keys on the way out the door, walking with speed to the Green Parrot. Halfway there, he realized he had left his phone on the charger.

"Crap," he said.

"Smooth move, Ex-Lax," Simon said.

"Jeez, John look at you," Kay said, opening her arms wide for a hug when he appeared behind her at the bar. Pilate smiled and embraced her, inhaling her familiar scent and squeezing her firm, athletic arms.

"Yeah. Old man," he said, laughing.

"Not at all," she said, looking him up and down. "Hey, are you working out?"

He nodded. "Yes, after I hung up today I hit the gym. Glad it worked."

She laughed. "Seriously, you look good. Marriage and parenthood agrees with you."

"Thanks, you too. I mean, you look good. Your hair is longer," he said, gently moving a shoulder-length blonde lock from her eyes. She blushed and smiled. "Really great to see you, Kay. You do look good."

She shrugged, her eyes glancing up to the right. "Looks can be deceiving."

"Oh?"

"Life off the force is good for me, I guess," she gestured for him to sit down. "Have a drink."

"If you insist."

Pilate ordered a Vesper martini, the complexities of which perturbed the bartender, while Kay signaled for another glass of wine.

"What, no gin and tonic?" he said.

She snorted. "As I recall, that's what got us started down the road to adventure last time."

"Lime sucking, some laughs and other things, yes."

"Seems so long ago," she smiled, her blue eyes darker somehow. She held the drink up to toast. "Malbec will keep me from sucking anything. To old friends."

"And to absent friends," Pilate said, clinking his glass to hers.

She nodded, eyeing him over the rim of her glass as she drank. Pilate noted dark circles under her eyes, hastily covered with makeup.

"So, where are you, anyway?"

"I went back to New York for a while, but it was pretty boring. Almost took a job as a deputy constable in my hometown."

Pilate burst into a staccato laugh.

"What's so funny?"

"Oh, you won't believe it," he said, taking in a mouthful of his drink. "I just wrapped up a brief, eventful tenure as town constable back in Cross."

She slapped his knee. "Get out of here! You? A cop?"

"More like a dogcatcher with delusions of grandeur."

"Catch any dogs?" she said, turning her barstool to face him.

"You could say that," Pilate said, glancing at her legs s they brushed against his. Her former assignment as a bicycle cop was still evident; muscular and pretty tan sticks, despite living up north for the past year or so.

"John, what?"

"What?"

"You just looked so, I dunno. Sad," she said, crossing her legs.

"Well, it got complicated."

"Dog catching can do that," she said, smiling and signaling the bartender over.

"Yeah, well, it was more than dog catching, I'm afraid."

"Oh, shit," she said, her eyes on his, steady.

"Yeah," he downed the rest of his martini.

"He'll have another," she told the barkeep, glancing discreetly at her wristwatch. "And can I get a gin and tonic?"

"Uh oh, Jane's gettin' serious," Pilate said.

"Tell me what happened," she said, her blue cop's eyes on his.

PILATE'S ROSE

CHAPTER SIX
Going Home Again

Heavens, is that a beer can convention? No, folks, we are at the corner of Live Oak and 10th, once home of school shooter Gary Rich—that's Neighborhood Watch Captain Gary Rich to you. Frequent guests of the Cross Township Casual Horror Ride will remember that John Pilate dispatched that weirdo without actually killing him. Pretty cool, huh?

No, John. You shut up.

You don't have to do this.

That's what they all say.

And here we are in downtown Cross Township. There's the VFW, the tavern where Craig Olafson—may he rot in hell —knocked our hero out cold, the café, Cusack's Cross and Cork B&B, and the town constable's office, with more holes in it than a fifty-ton block of Swiss cheese. You don't see that just anywhere, folks! Don't forget, John Pilate was even the town constable there. Technically he still is.

The rain is coming, John. Go home.

Within the hour, Kay was up to speed on John's life. She knew about the violence with the "hillbilly mafia" back in Cross, his current legal battle with Frechette and the strain on his marriage.

"Jesus, all we've done is talk about me," Pilate said, finishing his second martini. Kay had barely touched her g and t.

"Oh, well like I said, I'm here to get my affairs in order," she smiled, demurely, running a hand through her hair.

"So, it's like that?"

"You remember I had had a friend, right before I met you. She and I. We were…close."

"So, I ruined you on men forever?" he said, leaning on an elbow and waggling his eyebrows.

"Oh, good god, John," she sighed, a trace of irritation in her exhale.

"Sorry," he sat up straight and gestured with his glass. "These things loosen up my tongue a bit. So, what happened to you and her?"

"Well, she was somebody I knew when I was here on the force," she said, her eyes down, then back to his. "Dive instructor. Smart and sexy as all get out. We dated for about a year, and then things just sorta fell apart." She shrugged. "She's a real free spirit, and I guess you know the life of a cop isn't all that free," she took a sip of her neglected drink.

"She had other ideas about what was legal and what wasn't. Wanted me to get on her boat and move to Jamaica. I couldn't. I was devoted to my job and that was that."

"And that was that?"

"We broke up and she took off for Montego Bay."

"When was this?"

"About two months before you and me."

"Oh," Pilate said. "So I was kind of a…"

"Rebound?" She smiled. "Yeah," her voice softened. "But a wonderful one. A wonderful, messed-up rebound."

"Was I your first…?"

"Man?" she laughed. "Oh god, no."

Embarrassed, Pilate turned to the bartender. He looked bored as he shook another drink.

Kay's hand rested on his forearm. "But you were my best man."

He turned back to her, putting his hand on hers. "I am so sorry for what I put you through."

"What? The drunken sexcapades or nearly getting me shot and massacred by pirates?"

"Well, mostly for the latter," he said, accepting the martini. "The drunken sexcapades were a bonus."

She removed her hand and picked up her drink. "To drunken sexcapades."

They clinked glasses.

"Careful, John," Simon said. *I'm counting more than one gin.*

"I was sorry to hear your friend died," Kay said a moment later. "it's sweet you named Peter after him."

Pilate nodded. "Oh, thanks. He was one crusty son of a bitch, but he understood the most important thing."

"What?"

"That we're just passing through," Pilate said, looking at his drink.

"What's that mean?" she said.

"Just that we're all just passing through this life," Pilate said, softly. "That we have this one shot at things, and that none of it matters and at the same time it's all that matters."

She squeezed his arm.

"I guess that's been bouncing around my head a lot lately," Pilate said.

"That's not all," Simon said.

"What's up?" Kay said.

He shrugged. "Just restless I guess."

"Passing through." Kay nodded. "I get it."

Pilate smiled at her. "Don't mind me. I'm good. And I'm not looking for trouble." He signaled for another drink, avoiding her eyes.

Kay flashed a brief smile, then looked out over the Green Parrot.

"So, you have the condo all wrapped up?" he said, clearing his throat.

"Mostly, but I found out from Tom over at Key West PD that my ex's boat was in hock for unpaid dock fees and crap. She didn't want to mess with it in Jamaica—she had a friend who had a bigger boat waiting for her there, so she had rented it out to some dudes who apparently were about as responsible as the guy who leased my condo. Treated the boat like shit. Ran it ragged. Coasties found it floating out near Dry Tortugas. Not all that far from our little adventure on the high seas."

"Oh wow, I remember that little piece of real estate," Pilate said.

She nodded. "Good times. Anyway, there was nobody on board."

"Ghost ship?"

She sniggered. "You are soooo dramatic. Trailer park boat more like it. Probably some pot dealers transferred their stash to another boat and kicked mine loose. Don't know why they didn't scuttle her."

"Maybe they didn't abandon her," Pilate said. "Maybe somebody got to them."

"Could be. Not my problem," she shrugged. "Coasties found no evidence of foul play, just empty fuel tanks and a few dozen empty beer cans. Tom called me a while back and told me. So, I got the *Angry Rose* back and spent about a week over at Conch Harbor making her seaworthy."

"The *Angry Rose,* eh? Cool."

"Long story," she smiled, but Pilate saw it was closer to a grimace. "Going to give her back."

"Why go to all the trouble? Why not just sell her? Doesn't seem like your friend wants the boat anyway."

"She left it for me because I loved it so much, but I couldn't stand being alone on our boat. I want to give it back to her. I want her to know it's all good, you know?" she said, sipping her drink.

"You looking for anything else?"

Kay shrugged. "I don't know. I really don't. I don't... think so. I feel kind of lost right now, to be honest. I just feel the need to get things straight. I want to put things right with people I care about."

"Well, I'm glad we could see each other while you were doing that."

She glanced at him sideways. "I wanted to make things up to you, too."

"Me? Why?"

"I just never could tell you how I felt. You were in such a messy situation, and I was still bogged down with my feelings for her. I just couldn't commit to telling you how much I cared about you."

"Oh, Kay, come on," he said, waving her away. "You and me? That was all adrenaline and sex."

Her face fell. "Oh, that's all I was? Drunken sexcapades?"

"No, wait, that didn't come out right—"

"No, it's okay, John." She hopped off her barstool, a tad unsteady. "I get it. I gotta go. I have some stuff to do."

He grasped her arm gently. "Kay, wait, listen—"

She cupped his face in her hand and drew him closer, brushing her lips across his, then pressed in with her tongue.

He put his hands on her waist, pulling her closer. She pulled away, her lips breaking contact, her cerulean eyes wet.

"Be good, Johnny," she said, picking up her purse.

"Let me walk you," he said, fishing in his pocket for cash to pay the bill.

She shook her head. "I have to go. Bad idea. Ummmm… Take care of yourself. And get home to your family. This place is nothing but trouble for us both."

"Wait—"

"Just passing through, John. Go home to Kate." She cocked her head slightly and looked past him. "Funny how you married a Kate after being with a Kay. You have a thing for K-names?" she murmured a mirthless laugh and rushed outside.

"Kay, dammit, wait," he called after her, turning to throw three twenties on the bar. "Keep the change."

"Sorry, that's not anywhere near enough for this tab, bruh," the bartender said, shaking his head.

Pilate swore, took out his wallet and found a credit card, slapping it down. "I'll be right back."

He darted out into the street, his eyes scanning for Kay. No sign of her, she had melted into the crowd. He cursed and returned to the Green Parrot, sat back on his stool, signed the slip and downed the martini.

"It's for the best, John," Simon said. *"Drunken sexcapades are overrated."*

"Shut up."

"What bruh?" the bartender said.

Tipsy, Pilate ran the half mile to Kay's condo. The lights were off and there was no car parked in front. The run had gone a long way towards taking the edge off his drinking, but he was still confused about what just happened with Kay.

Pilate thought a moment about their conversation, how he didn't say what he meant. How maybe he said something insensitive on purpose to keep her at bay.

"No kidding, bruh," Simon said.

He paced in front of her door a few moments before knocking. She didn't answer.

She must have gone straight to the boat.

Pilate sighed, turned on his heel and started to walk back down the steps when he heard a deliberate clicking noise, the almost unmistakable sound of a semi-automatic pistol chambering a bullet.

"Put your hands up and don't move, asshole," a man's voice rasped.

"No problem."

"Shut up."

"Shutting up."

He felt a pistol barrel on the back of his neck. "I said shut it, wankstain."

Pilate nodded slightly.

"Now listen," Pilate noted a trace of the islands in his accent. "You're gonna tell me where your girlfriend is."

Pilate didn't move or say anything.

A sigh of exasperation drained from the man holding the gun on Pilate. "That means you can talk now."

"Oh, okay, as long as you're sure—"

The barrel pressed into the base of his skull. "No, no, funny writer man. No time for your use of them witticisms."

"I'll give him this," Simon said. *"He does make an effort to expand his vocab. Well, a little."*

"Check."

"What?"

"Right."

"Right, what?" the man rasped, apparently trying to disguise his voice.

"A… check?"

"Are you trying to be funny?" he said, speaking through gritted teeth and pushing the gun barrel harder into Pilate's head.

"Never. Trying, yes, but funny? Rarely."

Another sigh. "Okay, let's try this again Mr. Pilates—"

"Oh, now just a damn minute," Pilate said, raising his voice.

"What?"

"My name is Pilate. Pronounced like 'pilot.' Not like an exercise class," he said. "I mean, jeez, dude, you say you know I'm a famous writer or whatever, and you can't even pronounce my name correctly? Do you know how fucking old that gets?"

"I'm sorry, man, it looks like Pilates on the book cover on Amazon—"

"No hard feelings," Pilate elbowed the man in his belly, then turned around and blindly bit his crotch.

The desperate maneuver elicited a high-pitched howl as the man batted fruitlessly at Pilate's head with his gun. Pilate gagged knowing he was munching on the man's junk through a pair of polyester Bermuda shorts, but it was all he could do. He increased bite pressure on what he surmised was the man's testicles.

"Oh god oh god please stop! I quit I quit!" the man screamed. He dropped the gun and pried at Pilate's jaw with his hands.

Pilate bit harder, then seized the man by the back of each knee and simultaneously pulled his legs out from under him as he released his bite. The man hit the deck with a thud.

He moaned and rocked on the porch floor, his hand cupping his crotch.

Pilate spat and scooped up the gun. He checked it and saw the safety was on.

"This black-balled bastard was never going to shoot you," Simon said. *"How did you know?"*

Just felt it. The guy was scared. He's a lackey and not a very good one.

In the dark, Pilate made out that the man had shaggy black hair, a dark tan and smelled like pot. Pilate put the gun to the man's head.

"Okay, Sparky," Pilate said, spitting again. "My mouth tastes like your sweaty junk, and you're going to have to atone for that. No fucking around. Well, sorry to say you may not be doing any fucking around for a while. Pretty sure I crushed a testicle."

The man moaned, making a "fsssss" sound. "Shit. You really hurt me, man."

"Sorry. But you put a gun to my head, threatened a friend of mine and mispronounced my name. What did you expect?" Pilate rubbed his neck with his free hand.

The man continued to moan.

"Why are you looking for my friend? Why is she so important?"

The man's breathing slowed, his pain decreasing. "Ohhhh. Ahhhh. Fsssss. Okay, okay. I just got paid to find her and find out where her buddy dumped the thing. Ohhhh. Ahhhh. Fsssss."

"Stop making that noise. It's annoying. What buddy? What thing?"

"Her friend. Ohhhh. Ahhhh. Off the boat. Fsssss," he rocked back and forth, hands still clasped to his crotch.

"What did I tell you about that?" Pilate tapped his head with the gun barrel.

"Sorry."

"What thing?"

"The thing. You know."

"What, drugs?"

He breathed in deeply, made the "fssss" sound again and exhaled. "No, man. The thing was on her boat. She got the boat back from the Coast Guard. My boss wants the thing."

"Oh crap, John. This may be the real reason Taters used the code word," Simon shouted.

"What thing? I'm getting impatient, and you seem to have one ball left for me to mangle."

"No, man, no! I'll tell you what I know. Our people rented her boat to run weed and got hit by the Dry Tortugas by some other crew. They took the weed, but didn't know about the thing hid in the boat—the thing they stole from the woman. The other crew killed Lucky Jim and Ginger Martin.

The guys were transporting some big thing and got greedy—tried to sell some weed on the way. So the other crew took the weed and left the boat. Fsssss."

"Adrift. Why didn't they scuttle her?"

"Huh?"

"Sink it. The boat. You said they killed the crew and got the weed. Why not sink it?"

"When boss caught up to them, they said they were going to, but didn't get a chance to sink it because some big party catamaran was in the neighborhood. It spooked 'em, so they got outta there."

"God bless the *Rickroll*," Pilate thought aloud. "Go on."

"They threw the bodies of our crew overboard and got outta Dodge. I swear. That's what they told the boss."

"And what was it they didn't take that your boss wants?"

"I promise you by all that's holy I don't know, man," he said through gritted teeth.

"You're going to have a holy ball sack if you don't answer me," Pilate said, gesturing with the gun.

"Okay, okay," he said. "Damn, man, pretty hardcore to mess with a man's junk."

"Oh, really? And what did your boss do to the guys who killed your crew?"

"It weren't good," he whispered. "And he'll do it to me if I tell you anything else. Fsssss."

"Okay," Pilate said, switching the safety off. "I'm kinda ready to plead self-defense. I know the cops in this town, and am pretty sure they'll believe me when I tell them I shot you in the balls after you attacked me."

"Wait, wait! Okay, man, okay. Damn," he said. "I can taste blood in my mouth."

"You might want to get that looked at if you get away from here alive," Pilate said. "Now stop stalling and tell me what was hidden in her boat."

Upon further questioning, the man swore all he knew was something about a bar called Santa Margarita.

"What? How do you fit a margarita bar on a boat that small?"

"Fssssss. I dunno, man."

Holding the pistol on the man, Pilate called Kay's cell phone. No answer—it went to voicemail. "Kay, it's me. You're in danger. Please call back and let me know where you are. A guy attacked me at your place. I'm okay, but this is a situation. Call me."

"Man, you gotta let me go. I gotta get out of here. My boss won't be too nice to me when he finds out what I told you."

"What's your name?"

"James Jones."

"Whatever. Okay, Kool-Aide, you can go."

"Yeah, man!"

"Right after you tell me who your boss is."

"Damn, man. Okay. He's a guy, that's all I know."

"That's certainly…not helpful," Pilate said.

"Come on man; I gotta get off this island. I'm a dead man."

Pilate poked the man in the groin with the gun.

"Okay, okay! Fssssss. All I know is he has lots of commercial…interests in the Keys and the Caribbean. White guy. Rich British wanker. Always on the hunt for treasure and shit. Thinks he's James Bond or something."

"I need a name."

"Fssssss, man my balls—"

"Correction. Ball." Pilate pointed the gun at his crotch.

The man held his hands up. "Charteris! Mister Charteris. That's all I know."

Pilate gestured silently at the man, permitting him to go.

"Can I have my gun back?"

Pilate pointed the pistol at him. "Only if you take the bullets first."

"Damn, man, you don't gotta be like that," he said, hobbling off into the night.

"Well, John, I guess you know she's probably already on that boat of hers," Simon surmised.

Yeah, Simon. I know.

"And I suppose you're going to go after her?" Simon said.

Yeah. Just as soon as I figure out what a floating margarita bar has to do with this.

CHAPTER SEVEN
Pier Review

All right, fine. Keep driving. Ladies and gentlemen, this is the actual road where a henchman of Ollie Olafson—yes, that Ollie Olafson—drove John Pilate off the road, nearly killing him. But our John bounced back and Ollie, Craig and the rest of his crew are now asleep in the cold embrace of...

Pilate found a window that "Mr. Jones" had broken into and took a quick look around Kay's condo. Jones had tossed it, searching for something. No sign of Kay.

Pilate tried to use her phone, but it had been ripped from the wall. He climbed back out the window, made his way to a busy street and hailed another cab to Conch Harbor Marina.

At the marina, the night had made people scarce on the slips, the steady hum of sound from Duvall Street blunted by the tide.

Now to find the Angry Rose. He walked toward a couple of sunburned guys unloading coolers and fishing gear from a dual console boat.

"Hey, fellas, do any good?"

A heavyset man of about forty with what appeared to be a permanently red face looked up from a spilled tackle box. "Naw, got skunked."

"Sorry," Pilate said. "Say, I'm looking for a little boat supposed to be docked here. Called *Angry Rose.* Seen it by any chance?"

"Uhhh, no. Nope, sorry," he said, stretching his back. "What about you, Dylan?"

"Huh?" Dylan, a shaggy-haired, skinny kid of about twenty said as he grunted and carried a cooler off their boat and deposited it on the pier.

"Seen a boat called—" he looked at Pilate.

"*Angry Rose?*" Pilate said, looking at him.

Dylan bit his lower lip. "Huh, what kind of boat?"

"Not sure," Pilate said. "It's not real big. Maybe holds four or five."

"Angry Rose," Dylan said, scratching at his mop of hair. "Hmmm."

"She's captained by a very fit looking blonde gal, about yay high," Pilate put his arm out. "Nice looking."

Dylan smiled. "Oh, yeah. The *Angry Rose,"* his eyes flashed in recognition. "Yeah, I remember her." He nodded.

"Know where she ties up?"

Dylan looked up at Pilate. "Huh?"

"The boat."

"Oh," he said. "Yeah. She's one slip over, about midway down."

"Hey, thanks, guys," Pilate said.

"She a friend of yours?" Dylan asked.

Pilate turned back to him. "You could say that."

Dylan gave him a thumb's up.

Pilate waved at the pair and jogged to the end of the pier, crossing over to the other row of slips. Midway up, as promised, was the *Angry Rose*. No one on deck, but a light glowed in the cabin window.

Having no clear idea about boat etiquette, he stepped across the dock and onto the boat's deck, feeling the boat move with his momentum. He steadied himself and strode to the cabin door, raising a fist to knock on the illuminated window.

"Ahoy, there?"

Ahoy? Really?

The light in the window went out and the door jerked open, a 9-millimeter handgun gleamed in the dull ambience of the pier.

"Don't move."

Taters Malley put down his cell phone for the third time. His calls to Pilate were not being answered, and he was worried. *Had the cops picked him up?* They said they wouldn't cause a fuss if Taters brought him in. Besides, how sure was he the feds were monitoring his calls?

Hmmm. They would know he flew in, though. So that means...oh, shit. That means John and Kay are up to no good.

"Dammit," he said, just barely above a whisper.

"What's that, hon?" Jordan said, her eyes on the TV, where the Kansas City Chiefs were playing the Pittsburg Steelers.

"Nothing," he said. "Just trying to get John on the phone."

"Oh," she said, her eyes on the game. "You coming back? I think we've got the Chiefs on the run."

He nodded, grabbing a Modelo from the fridge and heading back to her in the den. Taters leveled his gaze on the screen, seeing only a blur of black and red colliding on a field of green.

"Put that away, Kay," Pilate said, his arms partially raised.

"John, you idiot, you know better than to sneak onto somebody's boat at night," she said, turning on the cabin light, activating the safety on the gun and putting it in a drawer. Her hair was up in a ponytail, and she wore a navy hoodie over a white tank top and black yoga pants.

"Man, I love those workout pants," Simon said.

"Sorry, I was worried about you," he said. "Can I come down?"

She sighed, poked her head out the door and looked around a moment, then gestured at him to follow her down below.

"Nice boat," Pilate said.

Kay was stocking the cabin's kitchen area with canned goods, bottled water, and gin.

"Thanks, it's just a beat-up Hinckley Picnic. I think she was built in the late '90s," Kay said. "She's seaworthy, but hardly has the creature comforts or speed of your pal's boat."

Yes, Taters' venerable and comparatively spacious Chris Craft Constellation, the *TenFortyEZ*, had the *Angry Rose* beat.

"Still, she's yours," Pilate said. "Well, for now."

She nodded.

"So," he leaned against the small dining nook table in the cramped cabin. "Going somewhere?"

"I told you," she said, continuing to put supplies away in the cabin's storage areas.

"Uh huh. And you're going tonight?"

"What makes you think so?" She said, over her shoulder.

"I don't know. You seem to have a …urgency about you."

"I told you I had to get the *Rose* back to my friend."

"With a gun?"

She sighed, stopped her hands and turned to him. "I'm a cop—"

"Ex-cop," he said.

"You carried a gun, John. You know you don't stop, no matter whether you're on the force or not."

"Search me," Pilate said, smiling.

"Angling for a pat-down, Mister Married Man?" She said, winking. "I don't need to. It's obvious you have a pistol tucked in your waistband behind you."

"Crap. Seriously? It's not mine."

She sighed wearily. "John, look, I'm not mad, but you gotta go. I loved seeing you. But go. Now. Shoo," she gestured towards the door.

"Can't do that," he said, sliding in behind the table and placing the pistol on it.

She implored him wordlessly to explain.

"I think you wanted to tell me more than you ended up saying tonight at the Green Parrot."

"John, I'm not going to screw you," she said wearily. "I don't have time for games, and you need to stop," she said, arms folded across her chest.

"Well, please do flatter yourself," he said. "Okay, truth be told, I'd love to get naked one more time, but yeah, I am married and also I have an aversion to being caught with my pants down."

"Oh? The wife knows you're here?"

"No, not exactly, but somebody who has been tailing you for a while is."

She rolled her eyes. "Nobody's tailing me, John. Don't be dramatic." She pulled a bottle of Jameson out of a cupboard and poured them both a couple fingers.

"Where do you think I got this gun?" He said, picking up the glass and nodding at the pistol. "I literally had to nut a guy who had it pointed at my head on your condo's front porch."

She cocked her head at him. "Don't screw around, man," she whispered, opening the drawer where her 9-millimeter was stored. "You serious?"

"Yes," Pilate said. "I can still taste it. Never mind," he shook his head. "I'd like to know what's going on, Kay."

Her eyes darted to the cabin door. She picked up her gun and walked to the door, locking it. She turned off the lights in the cabin and peered out the curtains.

"Kay," Pilate whispered, grasping for his stolen weapon in the darkness. "What's happening?"

"John, you need to drink up and get out of here," she said.

"I can't. Not until you tell me what's going on," he said.

"I have some…unfinished business," she said.

"No shit?"

"Yeah, and I think," she cocked her weapon. "I think you may actually want to hang around, now."

"What is it?"

"Looks like a couple of the goons who've been following me," she said.

Pilate crept behind her, craning his neck to see through the porthole over her shoulder. He caught a whiff of her scent, distracting him a second. He focused on the view and saw two men, one older and heavy, the other young and thin, walking the dock, each with a hand near his waistband.

"Wait, those guys were unloading a boat on the dock," Pilate said. "I asked them if they had seen you."

"Jesus, John, could you be more stupid?"

Pilate sighed. "Shit, I totally screwed up. I'm sorry."

"Dumb ass," Simon piled on.

"Alright, we'll discuss that later," she said. "We have to get out of here. That means untying the boat and gunning the engines into the harbor."

"How the hell are we going to do that? We have to go on deck and we'll be sitting ducks," Pilate said.

"Need a distraction," she said. "I can climb out the window above the forward sleeping cabin, and…I got it," she said, turning to Pilate in the darkness. "I'll crawl to the wheel, get out the flare gun and fire a flare off the bow. You run out and untie us while I get the engines going."

"Shit, that's a tall order," Pilate said.

"No kidding," she said, "But if we wait much longer, they're going to come aboard, and we're toast."

"Call the cops?"

"No time, and I'm not in the mood to answer questions."

"Fair enough," Pilate said. "You ready?" Pilate looked out the window again. "They look like they are trying to figure out next moves. Now's the time."

"Okay," she said. She brushed past him, squeezing his arm. "Good luck."

He nodded, squaring himself up at the door.

Kay hurried to the sleeping cabin, climbing over provisions she had laid on the bed and opened the small window. She crawled through, exhaling to make herself as small as possible.

She scampered through the window and disappeared from view. Pilate turned back to the dock, where the two men were creeping towards the boat. He unlocked the door, his weapon raised to the side of his head, pointed up.

Come on, Kay. Pilate listened for her footsteps above him. After an eternity of five seconds, he heard her sneakers gently scampering on the deck. The two men didn't appear to notice until she opened the storage locker and removed the flare gun—something rattled to the deck.

Shit. Pilate saw the shape of the two men look up, reaching for their weapons. In another second, Pilate heard a whoosh sound and saw both men's faces illuminated by the flare overhead. Pilate banged through the door, sprinting to the deck cleats. He shoved his pistol into the back of his pants and got the stern tie-off free, then carefully tracked his way to the bow of the boat, glimpsing Kay firing the engines.

A crack of gunfire erupted just as he threw off the bowline. "Go, Kay, Go!"

"Hang on!" she shouted. Pilate felt the boat lurch. He lost his footing and rolled to the edge of the deck, his right leg hanging off. Water sprayed his leg as the boat cut precariously through the crowded dock, angling for a straight shot out of the harbor and out to sea.

"John?" Kay screamed above the roar of the engines and stray gunshots.

With no energy to shout, Pilate held on, pulling himself with considerable effort over the edge and throwing his damp leg aboard. He rolled on his back and looked at the masts of boats as they sped through the harbor.

"You okay?" Kay shouted.

He raised a thumb's up, then clambered to his feet. Miraculously, the pistol was still with him. He walked back to the stern, then joined Kay on the boat's tiny bridge.

"They stopped shooting," he said. "But they had a boat two slips over. I thought they were unloading, but apparently, they were doing the opposite."

She nodded. "That's why we aren't stopping. They were planning to get me out on the water."

"Then actually, I'm not such a dumb ass."

She rolled her eyes. "We're heading out."

"Where?"

"Jamaica," she said, turning to him. She grasped the back of his head and pulled him close, kissing him. "Just passing through?"

CHAPTER EIGHT
The Wide, Wild Sea

Alright, fine. Keep driving. Ladies and gentlemen, this is the actual road where a henchman of Ollie Olafson—yes, that Ollie Olafson—drove John Pilate off the road, nearly killing him. But our John bounced back and Ollie, Craig, and the rest of his crew are now asleep in the cold embrace of...

Taters Malley shoved t-shirts into a duffle. "Where's my toothbrush?"

Jordan leaned against the doorjamb, raising a finger to point at his nightstand.

He looked at her, then the nightstand. "Oh, thanks."

Taters put the toothbrush, toothpaste, razor and can of shaving cream Jordan had set out for him in the bag.

"I think that's got it," he said, hands on hips, surveying their bedroom.

Jordan frowned. "Oh? What about these?" She tossed him a prescription bottle. He caught it—his cholesterol medicine. "Or these?" she tossed his nitroglycerin pills.

Wordlessly, he put them in the bag.

"You're due for bypass surgery in a week," she said, her tone flat, eyes leveled on his.

"Darlin', I know that," he said, moving closer to her. "But my friend's out there and he's in over his head—"

"When is he not?" she said. "Vernon, I like John, but he is nothing but trouble sometimes."

"You love John," he said, softly, touching her chin.

"Yes, but I don't love what he gets you into." She looked away.

"I'll be fine," he said. "I'm just going to go see if I can talk some sense into him. I'm bringing Buster."

"Oh great, anybody else from the retirement home tagging along?"

Taters smiled "Maybe that sexy Nurse Ratched."

Jordan cracked a smirk, and then wiped it off.

"Our intel says he took off on a boat."

"A boat? Why not yours?" she asked. "Why would he charter somebody else's?"

"Probably because he thought it would worry me, darlin', thus causing me heartburn," he shrugged, dancing around telling her everything he knew.

"You think John took off with Kay to…take off with Kay? No freaking way."

"Didn't say that," Taters said. "You know Tom at KWPD? He said he was supposed to meet Kay for lunch yesterday, and she never showed. Couldn't get her on the phone. He went by her place and nobody answered. They got in and it looked like somebody had got in through a window. Furniture knocked over, her clothes and stuff all over the place."

"Shit. You think?"

"Yeah. I'd say Kay is in some deep shit and our misguided, valiant pal John is trying to rescue her."

"He needs to grow up," she said, arms folded. "First the Steelers get destroyed by the Chiefs, now this. You have three days," she said, her dark eyes back on his. "Three, or don't come home."

"Honey, you don't mean that—"

Her stare never wavered as his eyes implored her to relent.

"Okay, okay. Deal. We will be back in Key West in three days," he said, picking up his bag.

"Okay," she said, turning to walk downstairs with him. "You have your gun?"

"Yes, dear."

Buster leaned against a pole on the dock beside the *TenFortyEZ*, wearing Bermuda shorts, deck shoes, and a colorful island shirt as he puffed on a cigar.

"Heya," Buster said.

"Where'd you get that shirt, *Magnum, P.I.'s* yard sale?"

"Ooh, I would definitely wear one of Tom Selleck's shirts—"

Taters held up a hand in a "stop talking" gesture. "Thank you, no need to elaborate."

Buster laughed, wheezing a little. "All right, all right. I know that makes you a little uncomfortable."

"No, I'm cool. You don't live in Key West for any length of time and have a problem with alternative lifestyles…just don't give me visualizations, please," Taters said, throwing his duffle on the deck.

"Fair enough," Buster said, climbing aboard. "Besides, Selleck's old. I like George Clooney nowadays."

The pair chuckled as they stowed their gear.

"Know where we're going?" Taters asked.

Buster nodded. "Tom at Key West PD said Vanderholt over at the marina told him what to look for."

"Why?"

Buster shrugged. "Well, that's the thing. It seems that somebody else had some eyes on the craft."

"No shit," Taters said. "I think our friendly neighborhood federal government had a hand in this."

"Makes sense. And Tom—well, the feds then—think he's heading to Jamaica, mon."

"Jamaica? Not the Bahamas?"

Buster shook his head. "Nope. Though I figured that would be where he'd go."

"I guess he and Kay have business in Red Stripe country," Taters said. "I like that almost as much as I do the Modelo."

"Convenient. So, how long 'til we catch up to him?"

"Well, I'd say that bucket they're sailing goes about half as fast as the *TenFortyEZ*, so assuming we match his heading, I'd say we can catch them just after they've disembarked at Montego Bay."

"Shit."

"Yeah," Taters said, firing up the Connie's twin Chryslers. "But you never know. John's no sailor. Neither's Kay, I reckon. Let's see what we can do."

"Aye, aye, captain," Buster said.

"You stock the cooler?"

"Does the Pope shit in the woods?" Buster said, cracking two Modelos as they embarked. By the time they reached open water, the pair had finished off two cervezas each.

The sun was sinking fast on the horizon as Buster plinked an empty can at Taters.

"What do you think they're after, Buster?"

Buster shrugged, then smoothed out his bushy gray mustache over his lined upper lip. "Not sure, other than Tom over at KWPD told me he heard a rumor."

"About John?"

Buster shook his head slowly.

"What?"

"About why Kay Righetti is back in town."

Kate Pilate tossed her cell phone into the soft cushions of the couch.

"Asshole," she hissed under her breath, jamming her hands into yellow dishwashing gloves and yanking a scrub brush from a pail of pink water.

She had seen enough blood in her life to prevent her from gagging. Instead, it made her angry. She scrubbed the floor, putting her back into the leavings of a would-be murderer.

Their two-year marriage had hit the proverbial rough patch, and she couldn't figure out why. Yes, John Pilate had issues; nevertheless, he was getting help, and the pair had survived their fair share of adventures to make things interesting.

"Damn house is cursed," she muttered, racing the brush across the floor, pink water foaming around it.

John's brief tenure as constable of Cross Township resulted in an accidental housecleaning of just about every crooked creep in the county, except for the kingpin, the wily Minnesotan Hilmer Thurman.

Thurman had gone dark since the night of the shootout at the jail. He was smart to fade out of view, as County Commissioner Jeremy Ryder was acting sheriff and looking for any excuse to arrest Thurman and make it stick.

No, that bit of drama wasn't fun for Kate, as she had to take up arms to defend her family. She couldn't be sure, but likely the blasts from her shotgun had killed a man. Maybe two. Perhaps she killed the brother of the would-be assassin who invaded their home.

But it had to be done.

Then all was quiet for a time. Taters Malley went back to Key West. Kate, Kara, baby Peter, and John settled into a calm routine after Pilate gave his badge back to Ryder. He had bad dreams and could be distant at times, but he was alright. The quiet routine of life on a farm town college campus helped them all.

That calm was decimated when the authorities caught up with Frechette. To her surprise, Pilate turned ever more inward. What started as relief that the guy who had absconded with the profits from his book was caught turned to anxiety with the civil suit. It was a nuisance suit, to be sure; one brought by an embezzler to embarrass Pilate by dragging out details of his personal life. However, it would go through while Frechette's criminal appeal continued. That could take months. And a whole lot of vodka.

John was going through a fifth every third day or so. He hid the bottles in an old barrel behind the barn, but she knew even without counting the empties. He had always "self-medicated" to a degree, but since the orgy of murders outside the jail and the lawsuit, she watched him succumbed to the urge to escape, to dull pain.

Hell, he preferred drinking to making love these days. Many a night he passed out on the sofa or the front porch swing, a hastily carved, dried-up lemon rind curled up in an empty glass nearby.

He wants to run away from a fight.

She sat up on her knees, dabbing sweat on her forehead with her forearm.

No, that's not fair. John runs right into trouble.

When a gunman took their daughter's class hostage, John ran into the line of fire. When Ollie Olafson and Hilmer Thurman's punks tried to muscle him, he didn't flinch when it counted. When pirates—oh my god, actual pirates—tried to kill him, Taters and…and that woman Kay, John dove right in after them.

Kate grunted, working at a dried crust of blood nestled in a crack.

But he runs from fights with me.

And now he was gone, diving headlong into something he probably lied to her about. He was gone, chasing whatever fresh mayhem he drummed up, and she could occupy herself cleaning up the blood stains.

"Fuck you," she said, her words drowned out by the sound of bristles on boards.

The water ran clearer now.

Kate stripped off the gloves and tossed them into the bucket, along with the brush. She stood, her knees complaining, and strode stiffly into the kitchen. She washed her hands and poured a mug of coffee.

Kate carried the steaming mug to the front door, kicking open the screen door. She sat on the porch swing, watching the cold October wind whip the Visqueen hastily stapled over the front window Ryder had shot out.

She stared for a long time out into the cornfields surrounding their little farm, her coffee gone cold.

"My cousins," Taters said, his eyes shining in the lamplight as the *TenFortyEZ* gently bobbed on the calm waters, cupping a Modelo Especial in his hands. "I visited them up north as a little boy. This wonderful little island up there in the middle a nowhere."

Buster nodded. "Good fishin'?"

"Yup, fishin' boat's where I got bit by the bug. My cousins took me out on their boat, and you might say I was hooked if you will pardon the pun," he chuckled. "It was the water and the way the boat cut through it. The guys smoking cigarettes and joshing and tending to the nets. Loved the sea from then on."

Buster sipped his beer, glancing out at the water, gesturing. "So you come by it honestly."

"I do," Tater said, tooting into the bottle with pursed lips. "But what I remember most is the potatoes. My, oh my, did they make great potatoes. I ate my weight in—"

"Taters?"

Taters chuckled, nodding. "Yeah, I ate them out of house and home, so they started calling me Taters. Mcleods. All Irish. Family called me Taters from then on out. Embarrassed me something fierce, 'cause I was in love with a gal. Even at that tender age."

Buster shrugged. "Shocking."

"Yes, she was something else, my cousin."

"Cousin?" Buster waggled his bushy eyebrows. Taters ignored him.

"Magical. There's something magical about that place, too. Dovetail Cove. All kinds of odd up there."

"Oh?"

"Oh yeah," Taters said, reaching for the cooler. "In fact, once my ticker is healed up, and we get John Pilate settled down, I may just head back up there."

Buster smiled. "I get it," he said. "My whole time in 'Nam all I could think about was getting back to the Keys. Never want to leave. Some places are naturally restorative."

"You miss Trev pretty bad, dontcha?"

Buster shrugged. "Don't do any good." He was quiet a moment, his expression taking on a softness. "But yeah, I miss my buddy. I was the reason he came down here in the first place."

Taters' eyes widened. "Wait, you mean you two were—"

"Huh?" Buster said, snorting. "Oh, hell no. Trev strictly loved the ladies, particularly his wife, God rest her soul. No, he just looked me up here after he got patched up with a glass eye after his discharge. Spent every penny he had on that shack he eventually left to John."

"Good guy?" Taters said. "I really didn't get to know him."

"He was one cantankerous son of a bitch, but yeah, a good guy."

The pair withdrew into themselves for a time, listening to the sounds of the waves and the hum of the engines as the *TenFortyEZ* made its way south.

"Take the helm a while?" Taters said. "I could use some shut-eye. Just follow the heading."

Buster winked and took the wheel. Taters walked to the back deck and took a seat in one of the fishing chairs. He looked up at the stars, casting his mind back to simpler days in Dovetail Cove.

CHAPTER NINE
Adrift and Afloat

John, why are you going to Monticello Cemetery? It's going to rain cats and dogs and all that place does is depress you.

Monticello Cemetery, where the aforementioned Jack Lindstrom met his death—indirectly at the hands of John Pilate. It's also where John and former Sheriff Sad Sack Scovill investigated a desecrated crypt, which held the remains of the parents of the man who is now his father-in-law. Need a program, folks? Can't tell the players without a program.

The *Angry Rose* cut through miasmic waters, parting the calm blue under the blushing rays of the waxing moon. The lights of Montego Bay winked and teased their proximity; the boat's fuel gauge coldly informed her that the teasing was cruel.

"Damn it," Kay said, tapping the fuel gauge with a knuckle. Why had she even come down south again? She still had a small scar on her forehead and a couple more on her legs and torso to remind her of that narrow escape from death.

"We're nearly out of gas," she said over her shoulder, brows knitted.

"Well crap," Pilate said, a hint of frustrated accusation in his tone.

"Wasn't my idea to leave without topping off," she said. "I think it's a safe bet that if we get in the sea-lane, we can flag down somebody to help us with some gas."

"Think our friends will try anything when they catch up?"

"We just need enough to get into the harbor, hoist a quarantine flag, deal with customs and get to T. She'll know what to do about this mess."

"If you say so," Pilate said, irritated that Kay put so much faith in a woman who created this mess in the first place. He looked up at the stars, as bright and warm as any night in Cross Township. It had not occurred to him until now that the one thing he loved about Cross was easily found in the middle of the sea.

He scanned the water behind them, looking for signs of the boat that had inevitably followed them for the last day or so. Nothing yet.

"There's Montego," she said. Pilate turned, the lights of Jamaica in the distance made him feel better. Not so alone.

"Oh crap," Pilate said.

"What?"

"No passport."

"Well, we'll just cross that bridge when we get to it. They'll probably make you stay on the boat."

"Good times."

Twenty minutes later, the engines sputtered, petering out about two miles from the harbor. She got on the radio and called for help. Running out of gas did not constitute a need for a full-blown distress call, but perhaps a friendly fisherman or the harbor patrol would hear and swing by with a gallon or two of gas.

"Hello, this is *Angry Rose*. We have run out of fuel. Would appreciate assistance," she said. She gave their approximate position and repeated her message a few times.

A heavily accented voice responded, telling her help was on the way. "Just fire a flare when you see ours."

The *Angry Rose* bobbed helplessly like so much flotsam.

"Looks like we're—" Kay started to say. "Oh shit."

Pilate turned back to the sea, spotting a boat's running lights closing on them.

"Probably just somebody with some gas?"

"John, I just sent the distress call three minutes ago. This is not help."

Both donned lifejackets and checked their pistols.

"Well, I always wanted to see Jamaica before I died," he said.

A flicker of light danced on the faded paint on the Skuba Due Dive Shack sign, catching T's attention as she loaded a couple of empty tanks and a busted regulator in the back of her rusted out Toyota Land Cruiser. Her tanned arm muscles rippled underneath a "Boob Marley" tank top, featuring a cartoon of the legendary reggae master ogling a pair of massive tourist tits.

She bought cheap shirts like this by the dozen from the shop at the end of the pier when they needed to make room for new merch. Nelly had taken a bath on the entire "Boob Marley" line of tanks and tees, selling them for pennies on the dollar to make room for more conventional tourist garb. T went through shirts pretty fast on her dives and endless days of sun, so Nelly's loss kept her clothed for next to nothing.

She ran a hand through her hair, scratching at her scalp. Years of seawater and sun had transformed it into something approximating straw. T couldn't remember the last time she had even bothered to use conditioner, let alone get it cut by a professional.

Damn scarecrow hair.

The waxing gibbous moon was partially obscured by clouds this night, but it still cast a glow. She took a moment to lean against the Toyota and look up.

Eight years in Jamaica.

Well, eight years in the Caribbean, actually. She had spent plenty of time in the Bahamas and Key West, too—though was a going concern in Montego for three years now. She and Romeo, her assistant, taught tourists how to dive safely, drink properly, and avoid too much touristy bullshit on their visits.

She liked Romeo. At fifty-four, he stood five feet, nine inches, all gristle, muscle, neon white teeth, and greying dreads to his shoulder blades. He always sang while he worked in the shop, and she could swear he sang underwater, too. Big Pato Banton fan, he preferred the early stuff.

A little Jimmy Cliff, too, mon.

She swatted a mosquito on her arm and closed the door on the Land Cruiser.

"Romeo, that damn light is still screwed up, we need to get it—" a burst of sound and light from the harbor drowned out the rest.

T whirled, her eyes focusing on a boat in the harbor, lit brilliantly by flame, pelted by burning debris falling from the sky.

"Jesus," she mouthed.

"Oh no," Romeo said, appearing next to her. "Not good."

Taters sprayed the last of the Glade around the cabin after leaving the head. "Whoo," he said, wincing. "Those dang canned oysters."

"Taters?" Buster hollered from above deck.

"I'm spraying, damn it," he yelled back.

"Get up here," Buster said, his voice flat.

"What?"

Buster said nothing, just extended the binoculars to Taters.

"Where?"

"Southeast," Buster said.

Taters scanned the horizon. "What the…is that a boat on fire?"

"At least. I turned on the radio and heard lots of chatter. A boat blew up near the harbor about half an hour ago."

"Oh, shit," Taters said, trying to get a good look. "All I can see is heavy black smoke. We're about four or five miles out."

"Jamaican authorities are telling everyone to keep their distance."

Taters handed Buster the binoculars and took the helm, throttling up the engines. "Hang on, buddy. We're about to run afoul of the Jamaican authorities."

CHAPTER TEN
Oblivion Or Not

That was another thunderclap, John—about two seconds after the lightning flash. It's getting close. Let's go home.

"There's nothing left of her," Buster said, his binoculars trained on the smoldering wreck as it slipped beneath the waves. "Just a couple Jamaica Defense Force Coast Guard fast patrol boats buzzing around."

"No...no sign of John and Kay?" he said, his face hopeful.

Buster shook his head, eyes downcast.

"Damn it," Taters said, the words catching in his throat. "What happened?"

"No idea. I'm wondering is why a boat like that, probably out of fuel or damn close, would blow up. Makes no sense."

"You think somebody helped."

He nodded. "Yeah, I do. I think the bad guys caught up with them. At least I hope they did."

"What the hell? Hope?"

"Yes."

"Why?"

"Because," Taters said, dropping the binoculars. "If the bad guys blew up the boat, that means they took John and Kay alive."

"Romeo, you hear anything?" T said, her lips wrapped around a Marlboro Light, eyes on the horizon.

Romeo stepped out of the Toyota, his face long. "Not good. Not good."

"They find her?"

"If what I heard from Skyrocket and Tandy is true, I tink it was the *Rose*."

Skyrocket and Tandy were deckhands who helped out when the charters got hectic; both had an ear to the ground and heard things at the social clubs frequented by "deckhands" for other charters.

She flicked the cigarette away and swept several empty beer bottles off the picnic table, shattering them.

"No bodies," he said. "Yet." Romeo stood still, awaiting her next outburst.

T raked her hair with her hand; her lips curled into a snarl. "What the fuck happened?"

"Not sure," Romeo said. "But it don't make no sense. Why would a boat blow up? The *Rose* was in good nick, right?"

T blushed, her face hot. "Could've been better," she said. "But it sure as hell wasn't gonna blow up without help."

"My pal Reedy's brother is with JDF," Romeo volunteered. "He said the boat looked like it coulda been rigged. But there's nothing left of her now. Burned to the keel."

T straightened herself up and looked at Romeo. "Close the shop. Cancel the charters. I'm going."

"Where?"

"You know where, Romeo." She said, heading inside.

"Then I am going wid you," he said.

T didn't argue. "Then make sure you're strapped. I never wanted this, but he's forced my hand. She went inside and picked up the phone.

"It's T. Tell him I want to talk," she said.

Taters sighed deeply. "Honey, this may not mean anything, but Kay Righetti was down in Key West, and we think—"

Kate bridled, inhaled and rose. "Where are you? Are you in Jamaica?"

"Yes, we will be here until we figure out what happened —"

"Is this number good?"

"Should be," he said. "Sat phone."

"I'll call you when I arrive in Montego Bay."

"Kay, you don't know what—"

"I am going to find out what's happening with my husband. You two can help me or—"

"Hey, hey," Taters said. "We're here. Of course, we will help. Can you just give us a couple of days?"

"It will take me at least a couple of days or so to arrange for childcare and get my trip arranged. But I'll be heading there if you don't call me in forty-eight hours."

"Okay, Kay," he said, wiping his eyes. "I'm so very sorry."

"Me, too."

"It could've been worse," Pilate said over his shoulder.

"I fail to see how," Kay said, grunting.

"Well, we're alive," Pilate offered.

"John, we're tied up in the trunk of a car, and it's only the fact that these guys are idiots we could get the gags out of our mouths."

Sweating from the stifling heat in the trunk, Pilate felt his cheekbone throbbing from the punches he took trying to fight off the dudes from the dock when they boarded the *Angry Rose* with a couple of buddies.

"At least we got a few shots off before they took us," Pilate said, punctuating it with an "ooph" as the car hit a pothole.

"We missed. Then you got beat up. Not exactly our finest hour," she said. "And those shitheels blew up T's boat. They're gonna be really sorry they did that."

"Uh huh," he said. "Some kinda badass, huh? So, look, assuming we are about to be dead people, how about you tell me what's really happening here?"

"I told you before," she said, groaning as the car traversed a thirty-yard stretch of potholes. "All I know is T was involved in something. Somebody used the *Angry Rose* to get at something important."

"Important to who?"

"Well, probably the guy who employs the assholes who put us here," she said.

"No shit," Pilate said. "But who else?"

"I don't follow," she said. "It's freaking hot in here."

"Focus," he said. "What about the feds?"

"Feds?"

"Kay, you know that we stumbled onto something two years ago in our little adventure with the Bigfoot. The little submarine out by the Dry Tortugas?"

"I'm thirsty as—"

"And you know the feds swore us to secrecy under penalty of a shitstorm of epic proportions if we ever talked."

"Yes," she said.

"Taters called me and more or less gave me the idea the feds were looking to discuss why the secret was out. It sure as hell looks like your little drama overlaps into mine."

Kay began to struggle against her bindings. "I gotta get out of here," she said. "I'm getting claustrophobic."

"Calm down, Kay. Just breathe normally and focus on my words," Pilate said, himself on the verge of panic.

"Okay."

"Okay, so your friend T…did you ever tell her what we saw in the sub?"

All Pilate heard was the sound of the car's suspension clattering on a dirt road.

"Kay?"

"I'm sorry," she said. "I—"

The car stopped.

"We'll discuss this later," Pilate said. "Just stay cool."

The lid of the trunk opened, but instead of sunlight, they were met with dim fluorescent light.

"Welcome to Rose Hall," a distinctly British voice intoned.

CHAPTER ELEVEN
A Bed of Roses

What is that? Sprinkles? Rain? Better go inside. Look at the thunderheads.

"Dylan cut their bindings," the British man said. "Mr. Pilate, Miss Righetti, please, make yourselves comfortable." Thugs pushed Kay and Pilate into a tattered sofa.

Pilate regarded the man. Fiftyish, white, paunchy, wearing linen and a haughty sneer. "Who are you?"

Flanked by his men, the man shrugged, taking a seat behind a desk in the dingy warehouse office adjoining the area where their captors had parked. "Is that important?"

"Charteris?" Kay said.

"Very good," he nodded. "I see your pillow talk wasn't strictly about who has the tastiest muff."

Kay rolled her eyes. "You do understand that I—we—are connected to some very powerful people, don't you?"

"Yes, I know you are a former police officer. In a tiny tourist town. In the United States. Well, I'm sure I don't have to tell you that you are not in the States anymore."

"What do you want?"

"You first crossed my path two years ago, wherein you incommoded me. By the end of that crossing, I was seriously inconvenienced by you; your subsequent activities in Key West absolutely hampered my plans, and now I find myself placed in such a position through your continual persecution that I am in positive danger of losing my liberty. The situation is becoming an impossible one."

Pilate smiled. "With a name like Charteris, I didn't expect you to crib from Conan Doyle."

The man smirked. "I'm no saint." His eyes flicked to a nude calendar, its pages ruffling with every pass of the ancient oscillating fan on the desk.

"Alright, I'll play along. Have you any suggestion to make?"

Pilate asked.

"Simple. I want what was on that sub. I want back what was mine."

"I didn't take it. The feds did," Pilate said.

"I am aware they seized most of it. But not all," Charteris said, a hand poked into his bulging waistband, as if bracing himself against pain.

"Really?" Pilate raised an eyebrow.

"Really. And Miss Righetti's lover has it."

"How is that even possible? Are we even talking about the same thing?"

Kay looked at the floor.

"Kay?" Pilate asked.

"T dived on the sub before you found it. She brought it up to the surface and took a few pieces as proof before she sunk it back to the sea floor to hide it. She figured after the government seized most of it, she would make a deal with Charteris."

"Pieces?" Simon said.

"Wait, but what about the guy who was after us in the first place?"

"He is no longer an issue," Charteris said.

"What? And you knew?" Pilate said to Kay.

"Not at first, really," she said. "I wondered, and finally she told me. It was the reason T and I split up. She lied and nearly got us killed."

"Well, where was she when we nearly got murdered out at sea?"

"Here, Jamaica. Hiding out."

"What a piece of—"

"So, you see," Charteris interrupted. "T tried to make a deal. She tried to arrange a transaction with me—I"

"And you double-crossed her," Kay said. "You nearly killed her."

"I'm appalled at your self-righteousness, really," he said. "After all, she killed my men. You and your lying girlfriend steal from me, and you're upset when I try to get back what's mine?"

"He has a point," Simon said.

"What do you want from us?" Pilate said, dreading the answer. "Do you expect us to talk?"

"No, Mister Pilate, I expect you to die."

"Oh please," Simon groaned. *"Pick a genre."*

"Tom at Key West PD says her name is Tammy. Goes by T. Owns a dive shop or something here," Buster said, turning off the satellite phone.

"And she is?"

"Kay's ex," Buster said, climbing into their rental car. "I have a sneaking suspicion she's at the heart of all this."

Taters looked around a moment, then discreetly slid the clip into his pistol. "So, we go put the arm on her?"

Buster nodded. "I see no other choice. And we better move fast, or else Kate Pilate will be here with a full head of steam. I heard what she did back in Cross when those goons had you guys trapped in the jail."

Taters nodded, grimacing as he turned his head and popped a nitroglycerin pill. "She's a gal not to be trifled with. That's the Taters Malley Theory on her."

"I always wanted to say that line," Charteris said, laughing.

Pilate reddened. "Hilarious," he said.

"Obviously, I plan to use you as a bargaining chip. You know all about chips, eh, Mr. Pilate?"

Pilate nodded. "Yes, the legendary poker chip. Whose idea was that, anyway?"

Charteris smiled. "Apparently Miss T couldn't resist a touch of the dramatic."

"I figured putting the coordinates in a poker chip was something a Bond villain type like you would do," Pilate said.

"I'm flattered," he said.

"So, we just sit here and wait?" Kay asked.

"No," Charteris said. His British accent was middle class, aspiring for aristocratic and not quite making it. "You'll come along as proof of life. You will do what we tell you to the letter or else this will not end well for you or your friends. Now, on the way over, you can be comfortable in the backseat of my Land Rover or you can get back in the car boot."

"Do we have your word we will be released when you get back what's yours?"

Charteris paused at the door and looked at him a moment. "Of course."

"I believed him, didn't you?" Simon said.

PILATE'S ROSE

CHAPTER TWELVE
Jamaican Jam

Thanks for joining us. Exit through the gift shop.
What's the most you ever lost on a coin toss?

"Shop's closed," Taters said, peering through the door.

"The Toyota leads me to believe she's still here," Taters said. "I'll go around back."

"Well, what the hell do I do?" Taters asked.

"Be conspicuous."

Taters flipped Buster off.

Buster peered into the Toyota on the way behind the shop. No dive gear or tanks, just a couple of backpacks. Gun drawn, he hugged the wall and crept toward the back, where he spotted a back door that he expected.

He paused and listened a moment, then started creeping towards the door. Two steps closer and it opened, shedding a wiry black man with dreads and a muscular white woman, trying to sneak out.

"Freeze," Buster shouted.

"Damn it," T said, raising her hands. Romeo raised his, dropping a large knife into the gravel.

"All right," Buster started to say, interrupted by Taters who appeared on the other side of the building's back door. "Anybody else in there?"

The pair said nothing.

"Look, we don't have time for this," Buster said. "We think Kay and John may still be alive, and we need to know where to find them."

T looked at Buster, then Taters. "You're not with Charteris?"

"Who's that?" Taters said.

"You guys do look a little long in the tooth to be wid him," Romeo said.

"You don't have to get personal," Taters said.

"Look," Buster said. "Your friend Kay has our friend John in some deep shit—"

"Oh crap, you guys again?" T said. "You're the ones who fucked everything up last time."

"Well, so sorry our near-death experiences inconvenienced you, little lady," Taters said. "Would've been nice if Kay had clued us in to your existence. So, would you kindly kiss my rusty butt?"

"Taters," Buster said.

"Well, seriously man, they nearly killed us, then we got freaking G-men after us, not to mention shooting up my boat —"

"Taters."

Taters made a face.

"As we were saying—" Buster started.

"We were just going to go meet Charteris. He's the one behind all this."

"Where?"

"We were going to meet him at Rose Hall Plantation," T said. "I'm going to give him what he wants in exchange for Kay."

"And John?"

"What-ev." T dropped her hands.

"Uh-uh." Taters gestured with his pistol. T raised her arms again.

"We're on the same side, mon," Romeo said.

"Well, mon, you'll forgive me if I'm not convinced by Miss Rat's Nest here."

"Hey, dick, nobody's talking shit about your grey hair —"

"That's enough!" Buster tucked his gun into his waistband. "Drop your hands. So, we will go with you to Rose Hall."

"Nope," T said. "He said just us."

"Tough shit," Buster said. "Do you even know they're alive? Where's the merchandise?"

"In the care of the White Witch," T said.

The Rose Hall Plantation is the grandest, oldest plantation in Jamaica. Spanning more than six hundred acres of sugar cane, pasture, and grass, Rose Hall is legendary for its history of slavery, cruelty, and purported murders. Johnny Cash once lived nearby and wrote a song about the White Witch, who is alleged to be the ghost of murderess Annie

Palmer, haunting the Jamaican Georgian style mansion and grounds.

"Why there?" Taters asked.

T shrugged. "It's a tourist trap. We can conduct our business with less chance of getting killed if we're out in the open—though he said he wants to meet there at dusk, between when the day tourists stop and before the ghost tours begin."

"Odd," Buster said.

"This dick has a taste for melodrama," T said. "He thinks he's a damn James Bond villain."

"Where's he get his money?" Taters asked.

"Not sure," T said. "I hear he's into treasure, which is why he was transporting this merchandise in the first place. Trying to evade customs."

"Treasure? The sub wasn't transporting treasure from what I could— "

"One man's treasure," T said. "Okay, we're supposed to meet them behind the plantation by the Witch's tomb at dusk."

"Cheery," Taters said, looking down at his shirt. "Good lord, is it always this damn humid here? I've sweated through my shirt."

"Maybe it's nervous sweat," Romeo said, smiling.

"Whatever, Boob Marley."

Charteris climbed out of the Land Rover and faced them. "Mr. Pilate, Miss Righetti, do exactly as you're told. You are to stay behind me, and understand that Dylan here will have a weapon ready to handle any indiscreet activities."

"Sidney Greenstreet here is getting on my nerves," Simon whispered.

"Dylan, watch them."

"Yep," he said.

The stone edifice of the Rose Hall Plantation, crowning a hill, reflected a bright white cast, even in the declining sun. A dozen or so tourists took turns posing for photos on the dramatic stairs leading to the front entrance as uniformed staff gently shooed them towards the waiting bus to take them back to one of the myriad inclusive resorts dotting the Rose Hall landscape, hogging the best beaches.

Pilate glanced sidelong at Kay. She gave him a look like she wanted to bolt. He furrowed his brow at her in response.

"It would be easy to run here," Simon said. *"It will be dark soon."*

"All right, move," Dylan whispered. "Follow Mr. Charteris."

Charteris donned an elegant straw hat and dabbed at his perspiring face with a handkerchief. He looked as if he were going to climb the stairs but instead took a path to the left of the building, walking past a stone spillway towards a shady area behind the Rose Hall House.

In a glade near a large stone sarcophagus stood an athletic-looking woman, tanned skin with wild blonde hair, a cigarette dangling from her lips. She wore a faded t-shirt and shorts and carried a small backpack. She stared at the little tomb, wisps of smoke escaping her lips.

"T," Kay whispered.

"Quiet," Dylan said, one hand covering the small semi-auto he held in the other.

A few paces ahead, Charteris signaled for them to continue following.

Pilate scanned the area, observing that tourists had vacated this area. Two men wearing tour company t-shirts stood guard at the head of the path and near the plantation house rear entrance.

"Aha," Simon said. *"Keeping it clear back here."*

Pilate cut his eyes to Kay, who sized up the situation immediately, nodding slightly. He felt his pulse pounding in his head, clammy sweat soaking through his shirt. The sun was sinking fast.

"How the hell do you expect to get a leg up here?" Simon said. *"You're outnumbered, and nobody has any guns. They'll wait until dark when everyone is gone and finish you off."*

The group arrived at the edge of the tomb area. "Everyone, meet the White Witch."

"Oh, go fuck yourself," T said. Her eyes cut to Kay for a split second, taking in Pilate, and then went back to Charteris.

"I beg your pardon, Madame, I was referring to the occupant of the tomb at your feet. This is the evil Annie Palmer's final resting place."

T made a face that repeated her first utterance, throwing down the cigarette and crushing it out under her tennis shoe. "Alright, let's get down to it, okay?"

Charteris chuckled. "Absolutely. Just as soon as we move a little further away from this historic pile."

"That's not the deal. We meet here. Out in the open," T hissed.

"And so, we shall," he said. "There is no negotiation. Move." He nodded at Dylan, who jabbed the barrel of his pistol into Kay's back. Kay yelped in surprise.

"All right, all right, shitheel," she said. "Lead the way."

Charteris pointed at the path. "Everyone walk. We will go approximately one hundred meters up the path. Stop when I tell you."

The group stopped when Charteris raised his hand in a secluded area, a canopy of trees obscuring the fading sun.

T folded her arms across her chest. "Not sure I like this," she said.

Charteris grinned. "What's the matter? Afraid of duppies?"

"You have to believe in ghosts to be afraid of them," she said.

Charteris surveyed the group. "Well, Miss T, I know you know this young lady," he nodded at Kay, then Pilate. "And perhaps this gentleman?"

T looked pained. "Man, your shit's creeping me out. Can we just get to this, please?" She started to remove her backpack.

"Easy does it," Dylan said, raising his pistol to Kay's head.

"No need for that," Pilate said.

"He's right," Charteris said. "No need for that unless you try any nonsense." He nodded at T.

T slid the backpack off and held it with an outstretched arm towards Charteris. He stepped forward, took the pack and then stepped back. He winked at Pilate and Kay, then looked inside the bag.

"Yes, so precious," he said. "My precious!" Pilate couldn't tell if he was being funny or not.

"Alright Gollum," Pilate said. "You got it back. Can we go now?"

Charteris looked up at Pilate, closing the bag and slinging it over his shoulder.

"A pleasure doing business with you," he said, stepping behind Randy, who was to Dylan's left. "Dylan."

Dylan pushed Pilate and Kay towards T. "On your knees. All of you."

"You don't need to do this," Pilate said.

Kay gasped.

"You piece of," T spat before Randy punched her in the head. She fell to her knees, moaning.

"You bastards," Kay said.

Dylan smacked Kay on the head with his pistol butt. She staggered.

"I'm gonna murder every one of you," Pilate said, trying to help Kay remain standing.

"Please," Charteris said. "You were in over your heads the moment we met. If not for blind luck you would have been dead years ago."

"Well, he ain't outta luck just yet," Taters murmured from behind Dylan, throwing off the safety on his .45.

Dylan turned, his pistol raised. Pilate dove at him, fists clenched together, striking the skinny thug between his shoulder blades. Dylan lost his footing and pitched forward, firing a shot. Pilate rolled on top of him, scrabbling for his weapon.

"Don't do it, mon!" Romeo came forward, smacking Randy in the temple. He fell, unconscious.

Charteris started to turn away and head into the trees, running headfirst into the barrel of Buster's gun. "I don't think so."

Pilate took a sharp elbow to his chin from Dylan but continued to wrestle him for his pistol until he heard a crunching sound and a moan from Dylan, then a grunt and another groan, this one louder.

Pilate felt Dylan's body sag. He looked up to see T standing on his neck; apparently, she had jumped on it twice and was gearing up for another stomp.

"T, no, he's down," Kay yelled. "John has him."

Pilate scooped the gun from Dylan's nearly lifeless hand and held it up as proof. T stepped off, embracing Kay.

Pilate stood, looking at the shapes in the partial moonlight. "Well, better late than never, Taters."

No one said anything.

"Taters?" Buster said. "Oh no."

Pilate looked towards the path just past where he had wrestled with Dylan. "Taters, hey," he said, stepping over Dylan and crouching beside Tater's prone form.

Taters lay on his side, gasping. Pilate turned his head and made out a trickle of blood oozing from his mouth. He patted Taters and felt a wound, damp with blood, just under his right collarbone.

"He's hit!"

"Damn it," Buster said. "T, any idea how we get an ambulance out here?"

"I'll get to the house and call Ambucare. They can take him to Cornwall," she said, sprinting away into the night.

Pilate stripped off his t-shirt and pressed it against the wound. "Hang in there, pal."

"It would seem you need my help," Charteris said.

"Umm, buddy, you forget who's holding the guns here," Buster said.

"And you forget I own this place. Your friend will discover that no one will help her without my say-so. You want an ambulance, and you will need my help."

"Fuck you—"

"Buster, wait," Pilate said. "Terms?"

"Simple," Charteris said. "You escort me to the house; I will permit the call, then you let me go with my property. No harm, no foul."

"How can we trust you?" Kay said.

"You can keep my men—if they're still alive—here," he said.

"Hey, wait—"

"Shut up, Randy," Charteris said. "So, what's it going to be?"

"Buster?" Pilate asked.

"Let's do it," he said, uncocking his weapon. "But no funny stuff. We take you to the house, you call, and we turn our backs so you can leave. Deal?"

"I don't know—" Kay said.

"Tick tock."

"Do it," Pilate said, urgently pressing his makeshift bandage to Taters' wound. He checked Taters' pulse and wasn't encouraged.

"Not good, John," Simon said.

"Did you hear me, Buster?" Pilate shouted.

"Let's go," Buster said to Charteris. "We'll be back in a minute or two. Keep an eye on them, Romeo."

"You got it," he said.

"Charteris, I won't forget this," Pilate muttered, looking up from Taters.

"I'm mortified," he called over his shoulder.

"Shut up and move," Buster said, shoving the portly man down the path.

Kay knelt beside Pilate and Taters. "How bad?"

"Not sure," Pilate said. "The bullet looks like it went through him, but he's definitely in shock, and I think he may have had a heart attack."

"Jesus," she said.

"Yeah," Pilate said.

Kay checked his pulse. "Thready. He's in trouble. He's breathing, though. All we can do is apply pressure to the wound and keep him breathing until the EMTs get here."

"Damn it all to hell. This is my fault," Pilate said.

"You mean mine," Kay said in a whisper.

A breeze rustled the trees, wicking the sweat from Pilate's bare torso. It felt good. He closed his eyes, taking Taters' hand in his, focusing on his friend's ragged breathing.

"Stay, my friend. Stay." Pilate squeezed the callused hand, pleading with the universe for even the slightest reciprocal gesture.

"Hey," Taters said, his voice ragged. "We do okay?"

"Hey! We did fine. You did great."

"S'good, man. I have to say that…" his eyes fluttered.

"Taters?" Pilate said, shaking him gently. "Taters?"

"Could use a Modelo."

Pilate laughed at the distinctive sound of the Jamaican ambulance siren.

"I just hope it was worth it, John," Buster said, leaning against the wall in the waiting area outside the emergency department.

Pilate, clad in a hospital scrub top, stared into space a moment, then buried his face in his hands.

"John?"

"I'm sorry," he said, the words barely audible.

"Mr. Pilate?"

He looked up, expecting a nurse. Instead, a white, auburn-haired woman wearing a black windbreaker stood over him, a woman with dark hair, identical clothing, and perfect posture stood behind her alongside a man wearing a Jamaica Defense Force uniform.

"Yes?"

"I'm Special Agent Leigh with the FBI. This is Lieutenant Commander Anderson of the navy and Commander Meade of the Jamaica Defense Force," she flashed a badge. "We'd like a word."

"I'm waiting for my friend. He's in surgery."

"We are aware, Mr. Pilate. You can't do anything for him but wait, so if you please?" She gestured for him to stand.

"Go on, John," Buster said. "I'll be right here."

Pilate nodded and followed the trio to a small room with a cheap card table and three fold-up chairs. An empty ashtray and some fast food napkins littered the table. A small, burned-out coffee maker set on a little stand with Styrofoam cups, sugar packets and a container of powdered creamer in the corner.

"Would you like coffee?" Commander Meade said.

"Maybe, if you can get some," Pilate replied, sitting. Meade raised an eyebrow and leaned against the wall. Agent Leigh sat across from him while Anderson closed the door and leaned against it.

"Mr. Pilate, we have a few questions about the events that led us here," Leigh said.

"Me too," he said.

"How do you mean?"

"I just want to know why you felt the need to drag Taters into all this? Why didn't you just contact me directly? You know damn well he was pulled into this by me—"

"We did what we did," Leigh said, green eyes steady on his. "Because it was in the best interests of this operation."

"Operation? I see. Well, the only operation I give a shit about is the one that you better pray saves his life." Pilate stabbed at the rickety table with his finger.

"Please remain calm, sir," Anderson said.

"I am. I'm super calm. I'm like infinity pool calm. Just tell me what you want."

Leigh leaned back in the chair a moment, then glanced at Meade and Anderson. "Not much. Just what we asked for previously. This never happened. You never speak about it, you never write about it. You move on and we leave you alone for good."

"You'll forgive me if I tell you I think you're full of shit, won't you?"

Leigh looked down at the table a moment. "Of course. But we mean it. You have my word."

"Wait, we lost the merchandise, Charteris got away and you—"

"Mr. Pilate, you bought us some time. In a joint effort with the JDF," she nodded at Meade, who nodded back, "we captured Mr. Charteris at Sanger. His Gulfstream was next to go on the runway."

"What about the—"

"Merchandise? We have it. It's safe and no longer a threat to anyone," Leigh said.

"I'm confused—this British bastard seemed to be after some kind of treasure. Gold bars. That wasn't what was in the sub—"

"Of course, it was," Leigh said. "And we appreciate your help. Had you not slowed him down—"

"Taters Malley is not a damn speed bump, lady. He's a human being. He's my friend."

She nodded. "And an American citizen. That's why as soon as he is stable we will fly him to the best hospital in Miami. All expenses paid by Uncle Sam."

"That's...decent of you. What about T and Kay?"

"Both will answer to theft and conspiracy charges, though I think Ms. Righetti will get a slap on the wrist if she can keep her mouth shut. And for her friend, there is the matter of some dead men. Then again, her silence may buy her freedom."

"You really, really don't want people to know about that thing, do you?"

Leigh blinked, smiled mildly and leaned forward. "What thing?"

"How do we explain this to Taters' wife? To my wife, for that matter?" Pilate said.

"His wife will be told he was the victim of a mugging in Montego Bay."

"These tings happen," Meade said, shrugging.

"What do I tell my wife?"

Leigh bit her lip. "That's your business."

"Thanks," Pilate said, standing. "Really."

CHAPTER THIRTEEN
Lost At Sea

John? John, can you hear me?
Let me out.

An hour after the jet took off with Taters and Buster for Miami; Pilate sat on the humid dock beside the *TenFortyEZ*, a satellite phone to his ear.

"I'm really sorry, Kate," Pilate said.

"For what? The lying? The danger you put yourself and your friends in? For shacking up with that—"

"I never shacked—"

"Just shut up, John. For once, just shut up, would you?"

"Okay."

"I'll make this short and simple. In a few minutes, I'm putting the kids on the phone."

"I know, and I'll tell them I will be home as soon as I get the *TenFortyEZ* back to Key West for Taters."

"And then you're going to say goodbye."

"What the hell does that mean?"

She sighed. "It means, John, that I'm done. You need to get your crap together, and the kids need stability. That means you don't come home."

"Wait, what the hell am I supposed to do?"

"Your psychologist is in Key West, and I think your heart is, too."

He rose to his feet. "Kate, wait, we can—"

"Work it out? I'm not so sure," she said, her voice clipped and monotone. "At least not now."

"Kate, don't you love me?"

She breathed out and said, "I honestly don't know anymore."

"You can't take my kids away from me," he said, a wave of nausea swamping him.

"I'm not taking the kids away; I'm protecting them from chaos. If you want to get lawyers involved—"

"Oh, shit no, no damn lawyers," Pilate said. "Kate, this is crazy, let me make this up. Let me figure this out—"

"That's exactly what I want you to do. Go figure this out. Decide what you want out of life and we'll talk."

"How long?"

"As long as it takes, but I think we need at least a semester apart."

"A semester? Always the instructor, our Kate," Simon said.

The voices of Pete and Kara piped up in the background. "Okay, they just came in," she said, her voice trembling.

"Kate, just a minute—"

"No, not now. Just talk to the kids, then please respect my wishes and go get yourself together."

"But, everyone's gone. Taters is recovering, and you can bet Jordan won't let me near him. Buster's pissed. I'm alone."

"Not completely," Simon said.

"What about your girlfriend?" Kate hissed, just above a whisper.

"That's not true. And not fair," he said, standing.

"Don't make this any harder than you have to, okay? Oh, and Magnus Peck called. Frechette and Mann want to settle. Okay, here they are. Peter, Kara, come talk to Daddy."

Standing on the stern of Taters' boat, Pilate clutched the temporary paperwork issued by Commander Meade of the JDF that would get him and the *TenFortyEZ* away from Jamaica.

The *TenFortyEZ* seemed alien without Taters aboard—much like Trevathan's place in Key West still did after more than two years. However, he had a duty to care for the boat, just like the fishing shack.

The JDF had provisioned the *TenFortyEZ* for the five-hundred-mile journey back to Key West, and the weather report read calm for the next three days. All he had to do was point the old Connie in the right direction and keep out of trouble.

"Smooth sailing."

He didn't look back as he edged out of Montego Bay, carefully navigating the traffic as he put his best friend's most prized possession out to the open sea.

A day in, Pilate dropped anchor not far from the Southern tip of Cuba, bobbing in the sea lane in International waters. Another half day or so would bring him to the Turks and Caicos, then on to the Bahamas to hug the spotty islands until he made it to the Keys.

The autumn Caribbean sun warmed his face, the blue sky and greenish-tinged waters delighted him. Pilate closed his eyes, enjoying the radiation and gentle pitch of the waves on the boat.

Where you, Daddy?

He dialed up a Colin Hay song on the stereo, "Far from Home" and pressed play. Pilate stretched, stripped down to his shorts and sat in one of the fisherman's chairs on the deck, a half tumbler of Jameson in hand. He spied a pod of dolphin as they broke the water in the middle distance, a family at play.

"So, where you, Daddy?" Simon said.

The Jameson burned his throat; tears tickled his stubbled face. He belted the rest of the whiskey, blankly staring down the sun as it descended the ladder to the horizon.

"Just passing through."

Pilate dropped the empty glass to the deck, sprung to his feet and dived into the ocean, the water cool and welcoming.

THE END

John Pilate returns in

PILATE'S 7

AFTERWORD

John Pilate is human.

He is kind, rational, sometimes clever, loyal and responsible...until he's not.

Let's be straight-up: John's a rascal beset by anxiety, mild depression and insecurity, all manifested in his constant companion, Simon.

John and Simon are acutely aware that with every tick of the clock the person you were dead sure you were a day ago can appear an unwelcome stranger in the mirror today.

I know the feeling.

If you've read this series since the first installment (the one I thought would be a "one and done", Pilate's Cross) then you know John is a restless, troubled guy who is probably at his worst when everything is going his way. He doesn't trust happiness, is suspect of commitment and desirous of danger and drama.

No doubt, he is going to screw up. John will lose friends, make new enemies and cause pain to his loved ones.

This is inevitable, as John Pilate is all too human.

But aren't we all, if we're honest with ourselves?

Is it redemption that awaits John Pilate in the waters of the deep blue sea, or merely oblivion?

My gratitude to you, dear reader. This writing game is not easy, and certainly not profitable, but it has its rewards in the knowledge that I entertained you. I hope you'll consider writing a starred review on Amazon.com for me. It keeps me going and helps others find the series.

Special thanks to my friend, colleague, talented cover designer, and this go-round, my editor, Jason McIntyre. He is a damn fine (and oh my, prolific!) writer to boot; I recommend you check out his stuff.

Please check out my blog at http://pilatescross.com/ for details about my writing, appearances, podcast, and more.

Until we meet again…keep reading.

Alex Greenwood
Kansas City, MO
2018

Pilate's Rose written in Kansas City, Mo. and Laguna Beach, Ca.
2013/2014
10th Anniversary Edition, 2019
www.PilatesCross.com

Listen to the Mysterious Goings On podcast with
J. Alexander Greenwood on Apple Podcasts

PILATE'S SHADOW

A New John Pilate Mystery

J. ALEXANDER GREENWOOD

TODAY

"I made you something."

John Pilate's eyes fluttered.

"Guess what? I'm going to open the little door to give it to you. If you be nice-nice, you get more nice things."

"Nice-nice? Who are you?" he said, propping himself up on one elbow. "Why are you doing this?"

"We've been through that, sir," he said with a petulant sigh. "Now, do you want this or not?"

He didn't care what it was, knowing that an open access panel door meant some cool air would get in. That was worth more than gold.

"Okay, okay," Pilate said, rolling on his side and sitting up, the relative coolness of the atmosphere of the floor obliterated by the heat hovering just two feet vertically. He flagged as nausea briefly overwhelmed him, and his gorge began to rise until he willed it back down, swallowing intensely and painfully in his parched throat.

"Okay, sir, now you be nice-nice here and I will open the panel. Okay?"

Pilate tried to place the accent. It wasn't foreign, exactly, but there was something odd about the speech pattern. In their previous encounters, Pilate had noted the man's voice was oddly flat most of the time, but when he was excited it became an off-kilter approximation of the giddiness of a child. It was a staccato, honking vocal gyration, the aftertones of which unfailingly lasted about two seconds after each excited sentence.

"Okay, sir? Nice-Nice?"

Pilate gasped, realizing he had not answered verbally, instead he had sputtered, *"Okay, mother—"* in his mind, cut off by his captor.

"Okay, okay," Pilate said. "Nice-Nice."

"So stand back, okay sir?"

"Yeah, yeah," Pilate said, a lone bead of sweat trickling down his forehead into his eyes, as if he were at the gym. He felt itchy and dazed; the liter plastic bottle of lukewarm water he had been given last night was now nearly drained. It was hot in here, not quite like an oven right before you stick the frozen pizza in, but damn close.

The panel door slid back, a sliver of light cut through the soupy black cloud, accompanied by a gust of air – cool in comparison to the dead heat of his cage, but not refrigerator cold. With the panel open, he could just hear the faintest roar in the distance – the sound of a highway not too far away – but he could not spare attention to that right now, not with fresh air playing on his face.

"Jesus," Pilate whispered. "Thank you, Jesus."

"Oh, so now you're into Jesus?" Pilate's old friend Simon teased from inside his head.

"Shut up, Simon," Pilate rasped, subvocally. *Wouldn't want Mr. Nice-Nice to think I'm crazy.* "That goes for you, too, Jesus." Taking advantage of the momentary light from the doorway, he turned to peer into the dim shadows of the room. A worn and rickety wheelchair rested on its side in the corner, where Pilate had previously kicked it, the bucket to piss in set unused in the opposite corner. *"Not much liquid left in me,"* he thought. The urge to move his bowels or vomit had mostly subsided, though the cramps in his gut—a fun feature of heat sickness—was ever-present, a perpetual, hateful kick in the balls.

The panel door was four feet off the ground, a rough rectangle about a foot tall and eight inches wide. A three-inch deep ledge was set inside; Pilate made out the lumpy welds around the ledge he had previously sensed by touch.

"Hey," Pilate said. "Hot in here."

"Now sir, you're trying to lose some weight," the voice said, then the honking laugh.

"Ha, ha," Pilate said. "Seriously, I've had heat stroke before, and it's not good, okay? This could kill me—"

"Do you want what I made for you, sir?"

"If it's an air conditioner," Simon said. *"Or a goddamned Glock. Or maybe a bazooka, even."*

"Sure. But wait, what's your name, pal?" Pilate said, switching gears.

"I am trying to give you something, sir," the voice was dull and flat again, signifying...impatience?

"Okay," Pilate said, rising to his feet and moving closer to the panel and the blessing of a breeze.

"That's close enough, sir. Stop there, okay? Nice-nice!" Pilate winced at the pestilential honking.

"Okay," Pilate said, luxuriating in the relatively cool breeze from outside the metal box – he was pretty sure it was a shipping container—he had called home for...how many hours, now?

"Now you wait there," the honking laugh again. "You're gonna love this, sir."

Pilate was intrigued, but more than anything, he wanted to keep this guy talking and that cool breeze blowing.

"Why are you keeping me here?" he said, trying to sound curious rather than outraged.

"Please, sir, it is now the effervescent moment. I made it for you."

"What?"

"Shhh." A black nitrile-gloved hand, at the business end of a long-sleeved white shirt, darted into the panel, a single index finger making the "one moment" gesture, then darting back out like the tongue of some alien lizard.

"Oh for fuck's sake," Simon said…his voice strangely outside Pilate's head now…almost as if he were perched in a shadowy corner of the container, observing.

Pilate ran a hand through his sweaty hair and breathed the welcome fresh air in deeply. Besides being cool, it didn't smell as dank and metallic as this room he now called home. An oddly familiar *chokka chokka* sound filtered inside the room along with the cool air, chased by silence.

"Oh, come on. It can't be," Simon said.

"Ta-da!" The hand reappeared, holding a glass containing a clear liquid cold enough to make it glisten with sweat. Pilate chuckled at the thought of a glass sweating as much as he was.

With a flourish, the gloved hand placed the glass on the ledge and withdrew.

"Somewhere between a martini glass and a coupe, the Nick and Nora glass, named after the cinematic husband-and-wife detective team," the man said, apparently reading. "It brings back the suave sophistication of 1930s high life." He broke out into more honking.

"Oh my god," Pilate said. It was indeed a martini glass. It was also his favorite style, the Nick and Nora model, featured in the *Thin Man* series with William Powell and the sexiest woman who ever lived, Myrna Loy.

"Please, drink, sir!" with the honking punctuated by nitrile-skinned hand claps.

"What is it?"

"Martini, sir. Of course!" *Honk, honk, honk.* "I made you a special treat."

"Umm, thanks. But the last drink I had from you made me sick and got me stuck in this box. Pass," he coughed. "What I could really use is a gallon or so of ice water."

"You please drink this special thing I made," he cleared his throat. "Drink it or you will not like the consequences, sir."

"It rubs the lotion on its skin," Simon intoned, ever the sardonically spectral spectator.

"I already don't like the damn consequences," Pilate said. "My name is John. Not sir. Now, I have been patient with you, but hear this, Mister Nice-Nice. Listening? People will be looking for me. Important people who are often tempted to violence. Get me? So you have a choice. You can let me out now and I will forget about this—"

"Like hell," Simon said.

"Or you leave me in here and my friends with the Key West PD find you and kick your ass from here to the Dry Tortugas."

"You drink my special thing or I will close this door and leave you here in the hot all day tomorrow." His voice was detached, flat and soft.

"What do you want from me?" Pilate screamed, his voice echoing painfully off the room's scorching metal walls, his face filling the open panel. He looked through the opening but saw only a bright set of work lights in what looked to be a hallway.

Hmm. Not outside.

"Special drink," two hand claps, one after each word, punctuating the way annoying people do when texting. "Getting warm."

"Fine," Pilate said, snatching the Nick and Nora from the ledge, swallowing half of the drink without hesitation. It was vodka, perhaps some gin and a hint of Lillet Blanc and lemon.

"*It's actually a passable Vesper martini,*" Simon said.

"You like?"

Pilate put the glass back on the ledge. "It's fine."

"Your favorite, right?"

"Yes," Pilate said, his voice barely above a whisper.

"Finish it?"

Pilate picked up the glass. "Maybe later. I'll hang on to it."

"You should finish it before it gets warm," the man said.

"What do you want with me?" Pilate said, his naked irritability waning with the cool air and the drink.

"Want?"

"Yes," he said. "Why did you abduct me?"

"We are friends now, right?"

"Who?" Pilate asked.

"You and me. We are friends now."

"If you say so, chief," Pilate said. "Is this what you do with your friends? Lock them in a hot box?"

"I just want something only a friend can provide," he said.

"Oh shit, does he want you to write a book for him?" Simon said.

"Well, tell me what it is, and maybe I can help and we can be better friends," Pilate said.

"I'm...I'm shy."

"Don't be shy, my friend," Pilate said, trying to smooth out the ragged syllables, his face hovering close to the panel again. "Just tell me what you need."

The panel slid shut, cutting off the sounds of the distant roadway, the harsh slamming sound painfully reverberating in Pilate's ears in the sudden silence.

"Maybe later."

Pilate screamed, seizing the glass and shattering it against the wall.

A Long Time Ago

"I made you something," the little boy said, presenting a piece of cardboard with both hands, his towhead mop falling into wide, dark eyes.

The woman didn't look away from the television. "Shhh, I'm watching this."

"Oh, well, I just made it to say sorry for—"

"Shut up. I'm trying to watch this," she jerked her head towards him, then back to the TV. "Well, never mind, it went to commercial and I missed it. Thanks."

"I'm sorry," the boy said, his hands trembling.

"What is that?" She looked at his hands.

He brightened. "It's a card I made to say I was sorry for breaking the knob on the radio."

Her eyes darted at the cardboard. "You're getting glitter everywhere. And that's not going to get you out of being grounded. Now go to your room."

"Okay," he gingerly placed the card beside her on the sofa.

She reached for a pack of cigarettes, knocking the card with glued and loose glitter and crayons spelling "Sorry" on the floor.

"God dammit, get back in here and clean up this stupid mess."

Last Week

The fist crossed his jaw, forcing his head back a few inches, jolting him into a strangely calm, split-second silence. His first impulse was to turn away, but that would expose a defenseless flank. Instead, he blocked his face with his fists to ward off another blow, leaving his ribs open for the stabbing left hook that stole his breath.

"Oof," Pilate gasped, staggering back on his left foot.

"Come on, ya bum. Get in there," Simon said, ringing a bell in his head.

Pilate reset his stance and fired off a jab with his left. It was a mile off, but he had to do something to try and slow down the incoming onslaught of punches.

Another fusillade of hooks pounded Pilate's ribs, driving him into the ropes, where he hung like a half-deflated mylar balloon entangled on a fence.

"Is this all you got?" Simon growled.

Pilate inhaled, inflating his lungs and pulling away from the ropes. He hopped on the balls of his feet, keeping his distance, breathing as deeply as he could through his mouthpiece and nostrils. He was having a tough time getting his lungs to fully inflate.

His opponent closed the distance in three steps, firing off a jab that glanced off Pilate's headgear. Pilate took the opportunity and landed a right hook, forcing his opponent to retreat. He followed up with a simple jab cross combo to the head.

"Get after it!" Simon bellowed.

Seizing the momentum, Pilate strode forward, firing off a sloppy left jab, right hook combo that landed, but with little force.

"Don't get cute, Rock!" Simon said. Pilate imagined Simon wearing a beanie and an old school hearing aid, cursing from ringside.

Pilate's opponent pivoted, ducking an un-thrown cross and punching him in the solar plexus. Pilate groaned, dropped to one knee and covered his face with both gloved fists until the bell rang. Pilate hauled himself to his feet. The rip of Velcro signaled his opponent was removing gloves with the help of a trainer.

"Good hits, guys," Felix the trainer said, tipping his hat to a lanky, greasy-haired guy behind him. "Erik, one: don't stand so close to me. Two: get them towels." Erik nodded like a squirrel with a nut and scooted away.

Pilate nodded, breathing heavily in the swampy gym atmosphere. The gym's website bragged about this being an old school boxing gym with no air conditioning. Pilate had thought that was somehow a plus at the time. Now he needed an inhaler to get through most bouts, his exercise-induced asthma more acute these days.

Felix pulled Pilate's gloves off. Hands free, Pilate removed his headgear.

"Nice work, John," Val said, removing hers. "I thought you had me there for a second."

"Right," Pilate said, his wrapped fist bumping hers, sliding through the ropes and stepping down from the ring. "I was lucky to get out of there on my feet."

Val climbed down, adjusting a black sports bra underneath her red tank top. "Technically, one foot, one knee. But you held your own."

Pilate made a face, his eyes heavenward.

"Let's get our miles in now and then you can go."

Pilate nodded grimly.

"Oh, stop pouting," Val said, swigging an orange concoction from her sports bottle. "You're the one who wants to lose fifteen pounds."

"Yeah, yeah," Pilate said, gulping from his bottle, then taking a pull off his inhaler. The lanky, greasy-haired man offered him a towel. Pilate shook his head dismissively. "No thanks." The man nodded and loped after Felix, who whistled at him.

Val shoved their boxing gear in a locker and tapped a few times on the screen of her sports watch. "You okay?"

Pilate nodded. "Yeah, my lungs are a little challenged these days. Mostly allergies, and exercise makes it worse. The inhaler helps."

She nodded. "Good. Ready? I'll take it easy on you. Here to Knight Pier and back. No stopping, no walking. Go." Val's athletic frame bounded out the door, her ponytail bouncing with each step.

"Hey, you're the one who wanted to go this whole 'Spencer for Hire' route. So get a move on, John. Simon says."

Pilate sighed and hit the street.

After the run and a quick bicycle ride home, he straightened the "For Sale" sign hanging from the old Trevathan place's porch. Pilate hated to let it go, as Trevathan had left it to the Pilate family; but it had not worked out the way the old man thought it would. The little cottage wasn't a haven for his family to escape to; it was instead the epicenter of mayhem, misadventure and marital distrust. If he truly wanted to get his family back, the entire island of Key West was a distraction he could no longer afford.

Pilate stepped gingerly from the small galley kitchen, chugging a Yeti Rambler brimming with ice water in one hand, a gallon freezer baggie of ice in the other. His old friend Trevathan's lounge chair groaned predictably under his weight. He placed the bag of ice on the top of his left foot, which pulsed with a stubborn case of tendonitis.

He set the ice water on the end table and reached for his MacBook. He opened his email and was met with thirty or forty new messages. He quickly deleted the come-ons to buy something and scanned a couple of others asking him to speak at the local Rotary club or donate autographed books to charity auctions before he marked them *unread* to deal with later.

A message from his mother and father remained in cyber purgatory, unopened days after it had first arrived. Another email from someone calling himself "Harold Strong" had a subject line that caught his eye: "Boxing Fan." Mister Strong said he loved Pilate's book and heard he liked to box. He wanted to buy him "a nice drink" and have a chat about his ideas of "why friendships are ordained by the universe" whenever Pilate "had an hour or two of free time." Pilate chuckled and wrote back: **"Maybe one of these days. Glad you liked the book, friend."**

A reporter with the *Miami Herald*, doing a story on leaders and powerful people suspected of having narcissistic personality disorder, wanted to interview Pilate about his long-dead nemesis, Jack Lindstrom. He hit 'reply' and typed out:

"Thank you for your interest in my thoughts. Jack Lindstrom was a damned nightmare for nearly everyone who knew him. So, I hope you understand I don't want to spend one more minute of my life thinking about him. Good luck with your story (Yes, you can print this.)"

Sending the message from the Herald reporter brought another e-mail scrolling onto the page, and the name "Kate Nathaniel" in the sender field made him catch his breath and sit up straight. It wasn't from her work account at Cross College, the one she usually used, even for non-business matters. This one was her old personal account, which she hadn't used much since they married. Or perhaps he didn't get email from her much, until lately.

Kate and John had not spoken in the two weeks since when she asked—no, *demanded*—her space and he gave it to her. He missed the kids and he missed her, truth be told, but he was trying to respect her wishes, as in, *"Get your shit together, Jack."*

"Shit coming together, babe," Simon said.

Pilate mentally waved off his inner voice and read the email. She asked for money for the kids' school clothes and to finish repairing the damage to their living room, still messed up from a home invasion a couple of years ago.

Kate didn't specify an amount. He toggled tabbed over to his bank account online and transferred $10,000. For once, he had plenty of money. His recently-recovered book royalties made him more or less liquid, and the pay from the occasional teaching or writing gig, as well as living in his deceased pal's "fishing shack," helped make ends meet pretty effortlessly. The most he spent on himself was on personal training fees and vodka...and he was trying to cut back on the potato juice.

Pilate read on.

"And since we are taking a break here I wanted you to know that Grant Fielding from the history department asked me out to coffee. I'm going to go. He's a friend—that's all, but I wanted to let you know because you know you can't do anything in this town without the gossips--"

Pilate felt his guts tighten, his breath became choppy, his chest tighten, accompanied by a tinny, piercing whine in his ears.

"Mother..." he muttered. He breathed deep after a few staccato breaths, starting the anxiety attack protocol Dr. Sandberg taught him.

"Where's the threat?" he asked himself. This began the calming process.

"Anxiety attacks can be headed off relatively quickly with practice, John." Sandberg had said. Pilate worked silently, breathing steadily, adjusting. Adjusting.

"Steady, John," Simon said. *"Where's that inhaler?"*

Pilate's eyes focused back on the screen.

"...gossips mouthing off. I just need a friend. You understand that, right?"

Pilate slammed the laptop closed and kicked the ice pack off his foot; it hit the wall and burst open, spraying half-moon-shaped pieces of ice across the room. "Take my damned money and go. I don't care."

Hot tears stung his eyes. He prowled the room a moment, then went into the galley, jerked open the old fridge door and scooped up a bottle of Tanqueray vodka in one rough gesture.

"John," Simon whispered.

He snatched a rocks glass from the cabinet over the sink and poured it halfway full.

"John," Simon whispered again.

Pilate slammed down a good swallow.

"John," Simon whispered.

"What?" he growled.

"There's Lillet in the fridge and half a lemon in cling wrap in the door."

Pilate downed the rest of his glass and strode out to the porch, swinging with a round kick that sent the "For Sale" sign into the street below.

"Wow. You look like shit," Val said the next morning, looking up from wrapping her hands.

Pilate grunted and dropped his bag. His head throbbed; his eyes felt like they had been rolled in fresh-mown grass clippings and jammed back in his skull backwards.

"Hey sunny, this one of those days?" Val said, her dark green eyes dancing under her sculptured brows, her ponytail whipping as she bobbed her head for comic effect.

He nodded, digging in his bag for hand wraps.

"Seriously," Val said, standing up. "Have you eaten anything?"

"No," he said. His chest felt as if it was bandaged tightly, the same feeling he'd had years ago, when he was shot in Cross Township.

She searched his red-rimmed eyes. "Yo, John?"

He glanced up at her a second, then went back to fishing for his wraps.

The bell clanged; two people began sparring in the ring behind them. Pilate stopped a moment, watching the clumsy ballet as the pair bobbed, weaved and punched—mostly striking the almost visible, humid air.

"We're, uhhhh, not boxing today," Val said. "As much as I think you want to hit something, we're going to do something else."

Pilate didn't argue as she stripped off her wraps and dropped them in her bag. "Come on."

The coffee's aroma dazed him for a second; John detected traces of hazelnut wafting past him as he sat on the deck outside, idly watching Val through the window as she ordered their coffee at Frenchie's Cafe, a tiny bistro housed in a white cottage with blue trim, next door to the Southernmost Inn, in turn, not far from the iconic Southernmost Point buoy.

Val's tanned, compact, muscular frame moved efficiently past two other customers, through the tiny cafe out to the porch overlooking United Street. Pilate pegged her at about thirty, though with her rich brown hair and vibrant bronze skin, she could easily pass for younger. He rarely saw her wear makeup at the gym, of course. And she didn't need it. Pilate admired her matter-of-fact ways, and could even tolerate that she was really into playing country music during workouts. She was just getting over a breakup with a cop.

"Total jerkface," he remembered her saying once in passing. "Turned out to be a real lunk on a power trip."

Lunk or not, Pilate couldn't comprehend how a guy could allow himself to lose a woman like Val. "She's the total package," he thought.

"Kate loves a hazelnut blend," Simon ventured from the recesses of his mind.

Val brought him a large coffee and sat across from him. "Croque Madames coming out in a minute."

"Nice." He nodded and picked up the coffee. "Thanks. I need sugar."

"I think so, too," she said as he took the coffee to the cream and sugar station inside. He dumped a few packets of the brown raw stuff in his coffee and gave it a cursory stir before returning to Val on the porch.

Val sipped her coffee a moment, looking up as several scooters, tiny engines cutting through the thick Florida Keys air like wheeled buzz saws, whipped down the street towards the Southernmost Point buoy.

"Thanks, Val."

"You look better already," she said, her smile revealing dimples and impossibly straight white teeth.

"Yeah, but in about fifteen minutes I'm gonna need to poop," he smirked.

"There's an alley," she said, jerking her head over her shoulder and returning to her cup, eyes on the street.

He nodded; his eyes joining her gaze on the horizon, looking south towards the end of America.

"I…had a kind of rough night," he said.

"No kidding?" Val's smile flashed, a perfunctory verbal jab.

"I uh, well, I think my marriage may be in trouble," his voice broke. He wiped his eyes on his sleeve self-consciously.

"Oh," she said. "How do you…I mean…what happened?"

"Got an email. She's apparently seeing somebody else."

"Oh my God," Val said, turning over the coldness of a "Dear John" email in her mind.

"Yeah, I mean, she just said that she was going to go for coffee with a guy."

"I'm confused," Val said, cocking her head. "Coffee. Like you and I are having now?"

Pilate stopped a moment, then slowly shook his head. "Well, I mean, it's different...here. What we are...doing. We're friends."

She nodded. "And this guy...he's not her friend?" she made air quotes.

Pilate sighed, then shrugged, exasperated at himself.

"Okay. Let's hold on to that for a minute," she reached for her coffee cup, then, stopped herself. "How long have you been separated? You never really said."

"About six months. I haven't seen her or my kids in three," he said, thinking back to a quick visit to Cross, where he picked up clothes and spent some time with his children. Kate had all her defenses up, full armor from head to toe, but he thought he felt some progress. They'd slept in separate rooms and all their energy and conversation was focused on the kids, but still. Progress.

And he had notched up his visits with Dr. Sandberg.

"Shoot, man, I'm sorry," Val said, her green eyes downcast.

He nodded. "I was...careless."

"Oh," she said, inferring something he wasn't sure he meant.

"Any idea what you're going to do?" she said.

"No," Pilate said. "I mean, I don't want to move back to that hellhole in Nebraska, but she doesn't want to leave. But I miss my kids and I was gearing up to move back when this hit. Even put the shack on the market. He looked out at the street at a flock of tourists walking past. "Now I guess I could still move back. Just be Mister Weekend Dad in a hellhole."

"Hmmm." Val sat back in her chair. "Maybe I should've let you punch something."

"How did it feel physically?"

"What?"

"When Kate told you about the coffee date?" Dr. Sandberg said, shifting in his chair, hands grasping a yellow legal pad and pen.

"Like I was having a heart attack, you know?"

Sandberg nodded.

"Well," Pilate cleared his throat. "I saw red. Like I could barely think. My pulse was probably racing, too."

"So was there a sensation in your chest or your stomach?" His open hand hovered over his chest.

Pilate leaned back in his chair. "Both, I guess. Not pleasant."

"Was it a radiating pain or—"

"Stabbing, then a tightness."

"In your chest?" Sandberg said, his hand dropping back to his lap.

Pilate nodded.

"And you couldn't think?"

"No, not really. Not for a few seconds. I got mad. I kicked a bag of ice across the room."

"A bag of ice?" Sandberg looked confused.

"I was icing my foot after a workout. Trust me, better the ice bag than my laptop."

The psychologist nodded. "So how long did this feeling last?"

"The nausea?" Pilate asked.

Sandberg nodded again.

"Probably the better part of twenty minutes. I drank some vodka to calm it down," Pilate said, looking away.

"Careful John, you tell him too much about drinking and you may not get to drink anymore," Simon chimed.

Sandberg made a quick note on the pad. "Did the drinking help the sensation go away?"

"I think it started to go away before the booze kicked in," Pilate said. "I felt short of breath. Sick, you know? And my chest was tight. Almost like when I got the wind knocked out of me trying to do a double play in little league. Not fun."

Sandberg nodded, standing up to close the blinds behind Pilate, then returning to his seat. "Then what?"

"What?"

"Once the feeling faded away, and you started drinking, what happened?"

"Not sure, I don't remember."

"Do you drink every day?"

"Used to. Until this happened I was working out instead. It helped. I wanted to lose weight. Vodka is a lot of empty calories."

"You want to lose weight—is that the main reason you started working out?"

Pilate twisted his mouth a bit. "Well, I mean, I guess I wanted to look better."

"Better?"

"For when I went back to Cross."

Sandberg looked up from his notes. "You were going to visit?"

"No, I was going to move back home to fix my marriage. I can fix it."

Sandberg looked at Pilate impassively.

"At least I thought I could. But that's not going to happen now." Pilate's hands trembled; his eyes watered. "I blew it. Stupid."

"I'm sorry." After a moment, he said, "You know, you say that often."

"What?"

"Stupid. You call yourself 'stupid' pretty often in our sessions," Sandberg said.

Pilate shrugged. "I guess 'cause I am."

He raised an eyebrow and thrust his head forward. "Really? Okay. Why do you think that?"

"Have you been listening to me the past few God only knows how many years?" Pilate said, raising his voice, trying to play off his frustration as a joke.

"Come on, man. You're a bestselling writer, a teacher, and a community leader. You've done some extraordinary shit—I mean you helped take down a drug cartel, for Pete's sake. I deal with lots of people day-in, day-out. I see what stupid looks like. You're far from stupid."

"I do stupid things," Pilate said, waving him away.

"I locked my keys in the car the other day—while it was running. Had to have my wife come home from work to help me. Does that make me stupid?"

"No, you made a mistake. Probably had your mind on other things."

Sandberg nodded. "You told me you got called stupid a lot when you were a child."

Pilate looked at his balled-up hands in his lap. "Yeah, there was a lot of teasing."

"Teasing?"

"I did stupid things sometimes. What does this have to do with Kate?"

"It's not about Kate. It's about you, and how you react to certain things. You're very judgmental of yourself. So they weren't teasing?"

"What?"

"Growing up. You just said you were teased…called you stupid. Then you said that you actually did do stupid things. Which was it?"

"They did the best they could," Pilate said, softly, looking at the shelf of autographed baseballs behind Sandberg. "She wasn't well," he said, rubbing his neck, eyes still on the baseballs. "Is that a Marlins ball?"

Sandberg nodded.

"I like the Royals."

"Mom wasn't well?" Sandberg said.

"She's better now," Pilate said. "You know."

"You have two kids," he said, looking at his notes. "Kara and—"

"Peter. You know that, come on."

"Do they do stupid things?" Sandberg raised his eyebrows, his eyes vaguely innocent, but Pilate had seen this look before, when he was setting a small trap in therapy.

"They're kids."

"Do they misbehave?" he said.

"Sure. All kids do," Pilate said, shrugging. "But they're good kids."

"Does Peter do stuff that makes you mad?" Sandberg said.

"Mad? No. Irritated, sure. He spills stuff a lot. But he's barely out of diapers, so—"

"Ever call him stupid?" Sandberg cut in.

"No," Pilate said, flatly, his breathing shallow.

"Ever hit him?"

"No," Pilate growled, glaring up from the fists in his lap.

"Would you want Kara or Peter to spend a week living in the environment you lived in as a child?"

"Stop pushing my buttons, god damn it. Don't talk about my kids, man." Pilate's chest ached, his vision clouded, his breath coming in short sips. He stood up. "I gotta go."

Sandberg rose to his feet. "John, are you okay?"

Pilate looked past him, hands raised, palms open. "Just let me go," he said, his voice breaking.

"Hey, let's sit back down and let you calm down for a minute," Sandberg said, his voice soothing. "We don't have to talk, okay?"

"I feel sick," Pilate said, easing back into his chair. The room was swimmy, his breath coming in short, ragged sips.

"Just breathe," Sandberg said. "Where's the threat? Breathe. Let me get you some water."

Sandberg opened the door, went out into the anteroom and brought back a paper cup of cold water. He handed it to Pilate.

Pilate drank the water and started to breathe deeply.

They sat in silence.

"I never hit my kids. You know I would never, ever hit a kid," Pilate said, the words navigating his tight lips. "And I never tell them they're stupid, or worthless or that I don't want them around. I am not like that and never will be."

"John, I know that," he said. "I just wondered if you truly did."

Pilate nodded. "What's going on in here, then?" Pilate said, tapping himself on the chest with his knuckle.

"We've worked on your issues for years, John, and developed ways to treat the symptoms. The panic attacks. I think we're at a point where we need to get to the roots of what happened to make you the way you are."

"The way I am?" Pilate said, wiping a tear from his eye.

"You have a form of post-traumatic stress disorder," Sandberg said.

"Really?"

"Yes, John."

"I think we suspected that for a while now, right?" Pilate sighed deeply, leaning back in the chair and finishing off the water. "From when I nearly got killed that first winter in Cross."

He nodded. "I think that event, as well as several others you have endured since then, have certainly made it worse. But you've been dealing with some pretty serious issues since you were a child. I think you developed defense mechanisms to survive some rough stuff that happened when you were a little boy. I think because of your mother's illness, you also unfortunately learned to despise yourself early and often."

"Wait just a damn minute," Simon said. *"Is he talking about me?"*

"I think this imaginary friend of yours...what's his name?"

Pilate shrugged, eyes on the floor.

Sandberg flipped through his notes. "Simon."

"That's my name, don't wear it out," Simon hissed.

"John, part of the issues you're having with PTSD, with your anxiety attacks, is that you feel them coming on and you get disgusted with yourself for having them."

"Well, I just don't think....I mean, it's not like I..." He trailed off.

"What?"

"PTSD is for people in combat, or firemen or cops. It's not like I've...I don't know," Pilate said.

"Earned it?" Sandberg said. "Most of my patients with PTSD got it when they were kids. I see a fair number of vets and first responders, but mostly it's domestic stuff. People who were abused as kids, or people abused by a spouse. Most of them think they don't really have PTSD because they don't wear a uniform."

Pilate sat back in his chair a moment; his temples throbbed.

"So, you don't fully acknowledge the attacks, John. You get mad at yourself. You despise it as some sort of inborn weakness. Over the years it got worse and worse."

"But I have worked on it," Pilate pointed at Sandberg. "With you."

Sandberg nodded, and put his notes aside, leaning forward with his elbows on his knees. "But John, we've hit a spot where you understand it, and you know how to calm down until the attacks pass, but you still press the ejector seat button and don't get at the full issue. Understand?"

"Not sure," Pilate said, taking a deep breath, then clearing his lungs noisily.

"It's a lot like Chinese finger traps," he said. "You know what those are?" He rose up and put his index fingers together, tip to tip, in front of him.

"Yeah. Got a pair at the State Fair when I was a kid. Chinese handcuffs."

"Okay, me too. Well, you know how they work. You put these on some unsuspecting person's fingers, and they get excited—"

"They panic."

"Well…sort of. Panic isn't quite the word---but okay. So they get excited and pull their fingers apart. But that does what?" He continued to act it out. "It only makes them tighter. The way to escape is simple. Just push the ends toward the middle. That opens up the ends a bit and frees the fingers."

"Yeah," Pilate said.

"Okay. So, your way of dealing with these attacks has been like that. You get so upset about having the attacks, that instead of relaxing and fully dealing with the situation, you get angry at yourself, and that only makes the trap worse. You almost literally beat yourself up for having an anxiety attack."

"Makes me feel helpless," he said, crossing his arms over his chest.

"And helpless is something that abused children feel above all else, John. There's nowhere to turn, usually nobody to appeal to. They just have to cope. Lots of kids create imaginary friends to help them get through it. Then, as they get older, they react to emotional stimuli like this in the same way they did as a child. It helps them survive, but that doesn't always square with being an adult."

"Says you," Simon said.

"And from what you've told me, Simon isn't always all that much comfort. He's your friend in some ways, but he's also a tormentor. He's reminding you of all the things you grew up believing about yourself, that you lack worth, that you are a bad person. This janiform existence isn't healthy."

"So I need to get rid of Simon?" Pilate said.

"Perish the thought," Simon said.

"No," he shook his head. "You just need to put him in his proper place. When an anxiety attack hits, you have to say 'hi' to it, acknowledge that it's happening, and work your way through it."

"I have been," Pilate said, exasperated.

"Yes, but you also have to tell Simon that you're okay. That he is okay. Simon is that little boy, dressed up in a big boy costume. You need to tell him that you see him, but his help is not required in dealing with adult John Pilate stuff. You need to be kind to him…just hand him an imaginary iPad and let him be a little boy while you handle stuff."

"Could I give him a martini, a smoke, and a copy of Playboy from 1983 instead?"

Sandberg smiled and nodded. "Whatever he needs to occupy himself. Just hand that stuff to him and tell him you got this. And maybe he'll stop with the nasty comments."

Simon blew a raspberry. *"Psychological double talk. You need me, Johnny. You always will. Maybe not today, but the next time the shit hits the fan, you'll be crying for your old pal Simon."*

Pilate cruised down U.S. 1, eyes drifting from the road to the azure waves being whitecapped by the high winds. His mind raced, picturing scenarios about Kate. Was she already seeing Grant, and the email was a formality to let him get used to the idea? Or was she sincerely just having coffee?

"Oh, Grant. You are so erudite and funny. I love the patches on your elbows!" Simon said, mocking Kate.

"Shut up, Simon."

"It doesn't help that he's better looking and smarter than you," Simon said. *"He's like Ryan Reynolds with a PhD."*

"I know. Shut the fuck up, okay?" Pilate growled internally. If Grant is so great, why is he teaching History in a tiny backwater like Cross College? Then again, legendary author Harley Cordwainer taught there, too.

"And your old pal Trevathan did, too. He was a solid guy," Simon said. *"And you nearly got him killed. John, have you considered that you really aren't good enough for Kate?*

That you got lucky and she married you then figured it out? You have it all wrong. She doesn't want to leave Cross. She wants you to leave."

Pilate winced. Simon hadn't been quite that hard on him in a long time. Apparently Sandberg had hit a nerve. He thumbed the radio volume up and rolled down the windows of the old Saab. He wished he had put the top down before he hit the highway. Just the wind in his ears and the sun on his face as he barreled past Big Pine Key back to Key West.

He had taken a day to run up to Key Largo for lunch with a friend of a friend.

"Hey there, landlubber," Ron said, his dark face nearly occluded by his floppy straw hat. He sprawled in a lawn chair outside his cabin not far from the docks, one hand working pincer pliers, the other holding a garish green fishing lure. Static-riddled Junkanoo music, pulled from a station in the Bahamas, played at low volume.

"Captain Ron," Pilate said, nodding at the lure. "Whatcha got there?"

"Green machine," he said, squinting. "Got bent by a perturbed Cobia awhile back." Ron grimaced, squeezing the pliers, then grunted. "There." He took off his hat, mopping his brow with a faded red bandanna. "Have a seat," he said, gesturing at another chair. "Just move my stuff over."

Pilate sat.

Ron eyed Pilate a moment, then put his hat back on. "How you doing?"

Pilate shrugged. "Okay. How about you?"

"Well," he lay a finger across his chin in an affected gesture. "The esteemed Union of Concerned Scientists say that by the year 2100, more than ninety-four percent of Key

West's inhabitable land will be under water, so I am also concerned."

"What about up here?"

"I imagine the scientists are also concerned about Key Largo in a similar fashion," he said, laughing and shaking his head. "Ain't that a bitch?"

"It is, sorry I'll miss that."

"Shit yeah. There's an upside to being old, huh? You hungry?"

"I could eat."

He grunted and smiled. "Let's hit the Fish House," he said.

"Let's," Pilate said. "I'm buying."

"Indeed you are," Ron said, chuckling.

After gorging on yellowtail and clam strips, the pair enjoyed a beer in relative silence. Pilate glanced around the restaurant's dining room, festooned with twinkling party lights hanging from the ceiling, fishing knick-knacks and pictures jamming the walls.

The waitress dropped the check on the table and collected plates. Pilate slid it in front of himself as Ron drained the last of his beer.

"Seen him lately?" Ron asked, eyes low, elbows on the table.

"No," Pilate said, fishing a credit card from his wallet. "You?"

Ron nodded. "Yup, he was touching up the paint on the *TenFortyEZ*. I think he plans to start taking charters again real soon."

"He okay?" Pilate asked.

"He's full of piss and vinegar as usual, but moving awful slow. That Jamaican affair was pretty tough on him."

"I know. It was..,..." he trailed off, his voice losing energy.

"The wife has him on a short leash," Ron added.

Pilate nodded. The last words he had with Jordan were more perfunctory than usual, and not kind. He brought the *TenFortyEZ* back to her from Jamaica, and asked to see Taters, who had recently arrived back home to recuperate from the heart condition that Pilate's last adventure had badly exacerbated. She told Pilate he was no longer welcome in their home, on their boat, or in their lives.

Pilate respected that, yet he missed his friend.

"You should call him," Ron said, watching Pilate scrawl a tip and his signature on the check. "Jordan has probably cooled off by now."

"Yeah, well I don't think I'm allowed to," Pilate said. "She said not to."

"Who gives a shit? She your mother?" He rolled his head around on his shoulders, as if trying to work out a kink, then faced Pilate. "Look man, you didn't drive all the way out here to buy me lunch because you missed me. For chrissake, you and I only know each other through Taters Malley."

Pilate shook his head slowly, his eyes on a Christmas light bulb flickering above the table. "I just want to know if he's alright."

Ron stood up, crumpling a napkin at his place setting, shaking his head; large, heavy-lidded eyes pondering Pilate. "Makes me no difference, but life's pretty short as it is, never mind having a bum ticker."

Pilate looked up at Ron. "Is it that bad?"

He shrugged. "Could be. Could be not. I'm just sayin' you gotta bury that hatchet. This is between you and him— not you and Jordan. Now, thanks for the lunch, amigo, but I gotta go see Rosarita about knocking the BBs off my neck."

"What?" Pilate said, rising to his feet.

He pointed at this dome before putting his hat on. "She gives me a nice shave on my head and neck."

"Oh," Pilate said, extending a hand. "Thanks Ron. If uh, if you talk to him?"

Ron sighed, hands on his hips. "I ain't your messenger service, JP, but tell you what, just this once, I'll let him know you asked after him." He nodded and winked.

"Thanks Ron, thanks a lot."

Ron nodded, slipping a toothpick in his mouth and easing away from the table. Two steps past John, he stopped and said, without turning, "Call him soon. I mean it."

A Long Time Ago

Johnny lay in a ball on top of his bunk bed, his hand drawing an outline around the cartoony James Bond on his *Thunderball* sheets. He had cleaned up the glitter as quickly as he could, choking back yet another "sorry" before retreating back to the room he shared with his brother.

Johnny climbed onto the top bunk. He felt a lump just under his Adam's apple, a hardness like a gobstopper had gotten stuck there.

He held his eight-inch Scotty doll from *Star Trek* in one hand, imagining Scotty in command of the Enterprise while Kirk and Spock were adventuring on the planet below. He seemed like a nice man, though he had a weird way of talking, and he was really funny when he had too much of what his dad called "the hard stuff."

In his other hand Johnny held a *Star Wars* action figure, smaller than Scotty-- - a beat-up Grand Moff Tarkin his older brother had once tied a tissue paper parachute to and tossed from the tallest tree in the backyard.

"You make things worse every time," the voice said, emanating from Tarkin's glowering countenance. It sounded like Tarkin's voice. Johnny thought Tarkin was a smart but mean guy, who also had a strange accent, but who wasn't at all nice. "I know," he whispered.

"Quite stupid."

"I know," Johnny Pilate said. "I have to quit messing things up and making her mad."

"You probably won't," the voice chided. *"Like she says, you're stupid, and you shouldn't even be here."*

"I can fix it," Johnny said.

"You always say that," the voice said.

"Leave me alone," Johnny said, rolling over on the electronic memory game he got for Christmas from his grandparents. It hummed and lit up different colored panels in succession, beckoning him to repeat the beeping sequence. Johnny didn't play with it much as a game, instead pretending it was Scotty's engine room on the *Enterprise*. It began the sequence, lights flashing tones beeping.

"Be quiet, Simon. Just hush up."

Today

Pilate roughed his dried-out, jerky-like tongue over cracked lips. The cruel headache that had set in hours ago, driven by gin and dehydration , pulsed behind his eyes. He sprawled, a couple of thin beach towels between him and the metal floor, his Hawaiian shirt rolled up as a pathetic pillow.

"This particular finger trap is an absolute bitch." Simon said. *"You have to get out of here. And pardon me for saying so, but I already read this issue of* Playboy *and I'm fresh out of smokes."*

Pilate lay almost motionless, a scant shiver running through him.

"Listen up, man. That froot loop thinks he's Annie Wilkes, and doesn't have the brains to see he'll kill you if he leaves you in this box."

"Remember my bunk bed? I was on the top bed so Kyle could have his Kristy McNichol poster taped to the bottom of my bunk?"

"If your brother only knew..."

"It was hot up there sometimes, by the ceiling," Pilate said.

"Yes. But harder to reach you up there," Simon said.

"Unless the belt," Pilate said aloud.

"John, let's focus on getting out of here," Simon said.

"You look like Peter Cushing again," Pilate said in his head, though chuckling aloud.

"Not a good look. Don't be a silly ass. I look like you, not Grand Moff Tarkin. I'm a much better looking, younger you, remember?"

Pilate lay there a moment, panting in the humidity.

"Simon, you gotta get me out of here. Go figure it out."

"Wait a minute, you aren't seriously suggesting that if I get through the wire…"

"I am the cooler king," Pilate groaned, sighing and rolling over, a sharp stabbing sensation in his left arm. "Dammit." He felt a shard of broken glass in his arm, and gently carefully pulled it out. "Thanks, Nora."

He gently padded on all fours, fumbling in the dark, finding the largest pieces of glass. Besides the bloody shard, he found the base of the glass with the stem intact and about two inches of sharp shard at the end. He carefully put it aside, against the wall of the container.

"Not all wounds are meant to harm," Simon said.

"Not all wounds are intentional, you mean," Pilate said. "Some people can't help hurting people."

"You really believe that?" Simon said.

"Some people are just screwed up. They can't help themselves. They just hurt or have some crazy itch inside that they can't scratch and they hurt other people dealing with it."

"You think that's what your admirer is doing?" Simon said, retreating to his corner.

"Who says I'm talking about him?"

Pilate signed a book, his childish scrawl marring the cream-colored paper, smiled, and handed it to the woman who stood before him.

"I hope you find it interesting," Pilate said.

The woman accepted the book from him and made a face. "Oh, I don't read that true crime stuff, it's too depressing. This is for my granddaughter."

"Oh," Pilate said, capping his pen. "Well, would you like me to inscribe it to her?"

She shook her head. "No, that's alright. She likes to sell these online after she reads them. It's best if it's not to one person."

"Gotcha," Pilate said, glancing over her shoulder.

"Well, I will move along," the lady said.

"Thanks again," Pilate said, looking over at the stack of books that was hardly dwindling next to his cup of cold coffee and a half-eaten brownie, courtesy of the book store staff.

"Cheer up, you miserable bastard."

Pilate looked up and saw a face he hadn't seen in years. Steel-grey hair and an off-center eye, clothed in a flannel shirt.

"Peter Trevathan?" Pilate stood up, knocking over his chair as he skirted the small signing table. Elated, he opened his arms to give the old man a hug.

"Can't do that," Trevathan said, recoiling.

"Why?"

"Because I'm gone," Trevathan winked, smiled and faded away.

Pilate opened his eyes. "Oh."

"You must be delirious if you'd rather have an old dead fart visit you rather than me," Simon said.

"I gotta get out of here," Pilate rasped, his words tumbling onto the dirty, hot floor.

Pretty Sure This Was Yesterday

"Meet me at the Hog's Snout. Six o'clock."

"That would be great, man," Pilate said, looking at himself in the nautical rope-framed mirror in his den as he spoke on the old rotary phone. His hand gripped the avocado-colored handset so tightly that his knuckles were white. Trevathan had never upgraded the phone, and Pilate liked it that way.

"Jordan's out at bunco 'til at least nine," Taters said. "I reckon that's plenty of time for you and me to murder a Modelo or two."

Pilate's eyes watered, a hardness in his throat made it difficult for him to speak. "I'm so glad. I…I didn't think, ummm…"

"What? Thinking you and me are through?" he snorted. "Not hardly. But we do have some serious shit to discuss, moving forward. Least of which is you owe me for some boat repairs. Jeebus, man, did you bring the boat home from Jamaica in second gear the whole way?" Taters chuckled.

"Oops. We'll talk. Six o'clock at the Snout. I'll be the guy in the Panama hat."

"Then you'll be the guy sitting alone all night. Just wear your usual hangdog expression, mister. I'll see you there."

"Deal."

"And John?" Taters' voice mellowed.

"Yeah man?"

"If you get there first, order some conch fritters and a—"

"Modelo Especiale. Got it."

"Good man."

It was only three o'clock, and Pilate had a little time to squeeze in a workout. He texted Val, who just had a cancellation. She could fit him in at four. Pilate sniffed his gym clothes, decided they weren't too nasty, double-checked his bag and headed for the gym.

Val was stretching when he arrived, her powerful legs accentuated by dark blue leggings, a pink Susan G. Komen t-shirt tied up to expose her midriff.

"Hey mister," she said, flashing a quick smile. "Ready to mix it up?"

He smiled back. "I'd like that."

"Well, no mercy today. No more nice-guy, got it?" She elbowed his arm.

"I'm in," he said.

They sparred for the better part of a half hour, then switched to a circuit of light weights and exercises. Pilate's lungs didn't love the humidity, but he kept going, sweat running down his face, his shirt and shorts nearly soaked.

"Okay, man," she said, toweling off. "Good workout. You really pushed yourself today."

"Needed to," he said, in between chugs of his Yeti. He looked at his watch. "I better get home and get a shower."

She looked up from her gym bag. "Oh? What's up?"

"Gonna meet a friend for a drink," he said.

She raised an eyebrow, smiling, then wrinkling her nose. "A girl?"

He was surprised at the question, considering he had just unloaded on her about his faltering marriage and his determination to "fix it."

His face registered confusion and perhaps irritation.

"Oh shit, John," she said, herself looking confused now. "I don't know why I said that."

"It's okay," he said. "Really."

She blushed. "I just, oh man. You just always seem like a guy going to meet a girl. I mean. Oh. Crap. Never mind."

"Hey, it's fine. And no, not a girl. Just a buddy I need to catch up with. Going to the Hog's Snout around six. Won't be out too long, he's on a short leash and has to be home by nine."

She nodded quickly, absently checking her ponytail, eyes fixed on the empty boxing ring. "Well, have fun."

Pilate sensed an odd unease with Val, but wasn't sure what brought it on. "Okay."

Val scooped up her bag, flung it over her shoulder and jogged out the door. She never really walked anywhere.

"Well, that was…interesting," Simon said.

Clusters of bright orange blooms adorned the Geiger trees near the entrance of the Hog's Snout, swaying in the humid breeze that wafted the scent of conch fritters, burgers and fries. There weren't as many trees and bushes these days; development had started to spoil the "outpost" feel of Key West's venerable Old Town. However, the booze still flowed, cocks still crowed and music still played.

Pilate had blanched when his friend suggested they meet there; years ago he had walked in on a dying man in the Hog's Snout men's room, after all. That bloody mess on the floor was always with him, and going to the Snout could make him uneasy until the drinks kicked in. Pilate was pretty sure it was yet another PTSD moment.

"Feeling triggered?" Simon said as Pilate looked past the restroom area and took a seat at the open air bar. Pilate distracted himself, checking out the hundreds of stickers, coasters, post cards and antique banknotes affixed to the walls and ceiling.

He was early; even if Taters was on time, Pilate would have half an hour to himself, sharing the place with a few dozen people eating and drinking in the various dining areas. This satellite bar had attracted only a couple of old conchs and a loud group of tourists congregated at a tallboy in the corner.

"What can I get you?" the bartender asked, wiping down the bar in front of Pilate and dropping a laminated menu.

"Pina Colada," he said. "Kidding. Can I get a Stoli rocks with lime and an order of fritters?"

She smiled back and nodded, eyes on the other side of the room. "Coming up."

Pilate looked around, self-consciously patting the breast pocket of his red *Magnum, P.I.*-style Hawaiian shirt, as if looking for cigarettes. An old habit when he sat at bars, even though he quit smoking years ago.

When his drink appeared, Pilate downed a healthy mouthful. He scanned the menu. Oysters looked good, despite his reservations about the effects of several recent Gulf oil spills. He sighed and put down the menu, deciding the fritters would do until Taters arrived.

He checked his cell for texts. Nothing. Pilate chewed his lip a bit, then typed

"Hey Val, thanks again for the great workout. Looking forward to our next bout."

"Oh my god, really?" Simon said.

"I just want her to know it's all good," he replied.

He sipped more of his drink, startled when his phone vibrated on the bar in front of him.

"I am so damn sorry man, Jordan staying home. Can't make it. Will call you soon."

Pilate felt hollow in his gut, as if he had been caught doing something wrong. He forced himself to breathe deeply a moment, then responded with a quick

"No worries, Taters. just lmk when you get some time"

He dropped the phone on the bar with a clunk and pointed at his glass when the bartender slid the basket of conch fritters and a tumbler of ice water in front of him. His phone vibrated again, with a thumbs up emoji from Taters. Pilate finished his first drink and moved it closer to the bartender's side of the bar and nibbled on a fritter.

After finishing off the second drink and destroying the basket of fritters, he needed to answer a call of nature. "I'll be right back," he said to the bartender. "Can we do this again?" he said, holding up his drink. She nodded.

"Want more water?" she asked.

"Never touch it," he said as he excused himself, stopped and looked back at her. "Hey, is there a different restroom— that one's not good for me."

She looked at him, uncomprehendingly. A tall, lanky man with greasy black hair haphazardly tucked under a sweaty Jimmy Buffet trucker cap leaning on the bar a few feet away volunteered that there was one on the other side of the restaurant. Pilate nodded in gratitude and headed towards it.

At the urinal, Pilate felt the back pocket of his shorts vibrate. After he washed up, he checked to see a text reply notification from Val.

"No worries, man. had a brain fart. got embarrassed."

Pilate leaned against the wall and texted a reply.

"Oh. I probably acted like I was bothered by it when I wasn't. Let me make it up to you with a drink. Come on over to the Snout." Pilate strode past the other diners as the restaurant started to fill up. When he got back to his seat at the bar, there was now only a couple of seats left open. His drink was waiting, the empty fritters basket collected. He took a quick sip and looked at his phone.

"I'd love to, but you have your friend there and u don't need a 3rd wheel."

The drink had him feeling good, further amped up by a rush at the prospect of hanging out with Val somewhere that didn't smell like Rocky Balboa's armpit. He thumbed his screen and typed:

"Actually, he canceled. Come on out. Don't make me drink alone."

Pilate scanned the bar, looking for a pair of seats together should Val accept his invitation. More people had trickled in, and this section was no longer as empty as before. Everyone seemed paired up, conchs and tourists alike, though the lanky man under the sweat-stained Jimmy Buffet trucker cap nursed a Bud by his lonesome.

Pilate's phone vibrated again.

"Ok. Tell me again where u are."

He texted back the info.

"Be there in 20 mins or so. SEE...U R DRINKING WITH A GIRL TONIGHT."

Pilate chuckled and texted back a laughing face emoji, then put his phone down and drank more of his vodka. He felt excited about seeing Val socially like this, but didn't really have any assumptions it was anything more than two friends having a drink. He also felt a little guilty, but the vodka was translating that into self-righteousness just fine, thanks. "If she can have coffee with Deadpool McDreamy, I can have a drink with my personal trainer."

A few moments later, he felt a mild wave of nausea roll over him. "Ugh, not now," he thought as his bowels cramped up.

"Maybe you should have had the oysters after all," Simon said.

The cramps came faster and more forcefully; sweat broke out on his forehead. Pilate signaled the bartender. "Hey, I have a friend joining me, can you hold my place here while I go comb my hair?"

The bartender looked annoyed. "What?"

"Just please hold my seat while I go to the can, okay? You have my credit card. My friend, her name is Val. She's on the way."

She made a face like she wanted to say an exasperated "Okay!" and moved on to another customer.

Pilate made a beeline for the restroom of death he had wanted to avoid; he could tell that he needed to hurry if he didn't want to make a mess of himself and the bar. He made it inside; it took only an instant to realize the restroom had been repainted and perhaps even remodeled after the murder there a few years ago. Sure, it was still kind of run-down, but it lacked any sign of the bloodletting he had witnessed.

Blessed with an empty stall, he got there in time to lower his shorts and sit, only to realize he needed to throw up even more. Pilate managed to get back on his feet, pull up his shorts, turn around and vomit. Over and over, his gut spasmed, sending the drinks, fritters, and bile into the toilet.

The sweating and cramps started to subside, but he felt woozy and placed a hand on the cinder block wall. He heard a man's voice, oddly nasal.

"Hey sir, are you okay?"

"Hmm?" he said, losing his balance a little, trying to exit the stall but his feet kept wanting to twist underneath him. His chest tightened; a roar filled his ears. "I think I'm—"

All went black.

"Wake up, Mister Pilate."

With great effort, Pilate opened one eye halfway, it was dark and he felt sour, hot breath on his face.

A mild slap on the cheek. "Wake up or it's strike one."

Pilate forced his eyes open, taking in a silhouette of a tall figure standing in a doorway.

"Jack? Lindstrom?" he stammered, raising his head off the floor. "You're dead. I'm not playing this game again. I saw you die."

"Is that so?"

"I'm not spending one more minute of my life thinking of you, bad hooch or no," Pilate said. "You're not real."

"There's water in a bottle there, sir," the voice said. "It's not Parry-air but it will do." *Honk honk.* "We'll talk later. Get some rest." The figure stepped out of the doorway and slammed shut a steel door.

Today...Perhaps

From his perspective lying on the floor, the metal room was pitch black, save for a couple of pinholes of light coming through tiny holes drilled in the massive door. The holes were big enough to let in a dim, shadowy light, but not enough air to feel any breeze. He felt clammy; the atmosphere was again oppressive since his captor had slammed the access panel shut a few hours ago. He wished for a pull on his inhaler.

"You really need to work on keeping that guy happy so he doesn't close that panel in a huff," Simon said from the corner. Pilate imagined his old friend sitting placidly in the wheelchair, legs crossed, a *Playboy* on his lap, cigarette in his lips, his face in shadow.

"Definitely wish I had finished that drink instead of painting the wall with it," Pilate croaked.

"Yes, and now there's the broken glass to contend with," Simon said.

Pilate sat up on his elbow, one hand finding the large shard.

"That's probably as big a piece as is left," Simon said.

Pilate agreed silently and placed the glass at the head of his sweaty beach towel bed. He tried to make that end of the bed more pillow-like, manipulating the damp fabric into a bump when his hand connected with something that wasn't broken glass. "What the hell?" It was a smooth, familiar rectangle, about four and half inches long and a few centimeters in diameter. He scooped it up. "No fucking way. My cell phone."

Pilate instinctively felt for the iPhone home button, and pressed. The screen came to life, a photo of his children beaming at him, along with the date and time: 2:02 a.m. He pressed his thumb into the button, dismissing the lock screen and bringing up his familiar home screen.

"Yes!" Pilate said, dialing 911. The words "No Service" appeared at the top of the screen, and he felt the hope that had begun to break out die a lonely death in his heart.

"Damn it. Of course, there's no way a signal will get out of this steel box," he said.

"Yes, well, that seems to be the direction we're all going," Simon added. *"I guess he did hang on to your wallet though. Maybe he dropped it somewhere nearby too."*

Pilate ignored him and went to his text messages, thanking God he had set the font size larger only last week so that he could make out the text without his readers, which were sitting on his nightstand at the Trevathan cottage. He had five messages. A text from Taters arrived about ten minutes after his last text from Val:

"Hey man, I was out of line. I just told Jordan that I want to see you I'm not a damn child and she can't tell me who I can play with. See you in a few. Order me a Modelo. I'm fired up."

The next was from Val:

"Hey, where are you? I'm here."

She had followed up in five minutes with:

"John, are you around? Asked bartender. She said u not tabbed out. Where R U?"

Ten minutes later, Taters chimed in again:

"I'm chatting with your girlfriend, buddy. She's pretty cool. Better come back soon before I tell her about your wife. LOL Seriously where you at?

A final text came through from Val twenty minutes later:

"You're not home. Not at the bar. Are u okay? You have 10 mins to respond or I'm calling the lunk"

"Oh, I hope you did, Val," Pilate said. He thumbed his keyboard and typed a response to Taters and Val:

"I'm in big trouble! Locked in steel container I think - really hot in here. Crazy guy locked me in no water REALLY HOT. NOT A JOKE. I need HELP NOW. Don't know where I am. He's nuts he may abandon me Please don't let me die in here"

Pilate hit send. In a moment, he received the response:

"Message Send failure. Please check your network connection and try again."

"Oh goddammit," Pilate said. "Damn it. Damn it!" he shouted.

"Don't give up, John. This guy isn't so smart, leaving you your phone," Simon soothed.

"He probably didn't notice I had it. I bet it fell out of my pocket when he dumped me in this goddamned steel sweat lodge."

"All the same, he's not careful. And he's crazy," Simon said. "The guy likes Buffet and Bud light, after all. We need to be prepared when he returns."

"Prepared how?" Pilate rolled over on his back.

"Check the battery on the phone, John."

"42 percent," he said.

"More than enough. Turn on the flashlight app."

Pilate found the app and turned it on. The light shocked his eyes. He swung the light's beam around the container's grey, corrugated steel walls. Hanging from the ceiling was a cord and a broken light bulb. The floor was clean, save a few dust bunnies in one corner and tiny bits of broken glass from his martini just about everywhere. The wheelchair, despite the evidence of his conversation, was empty. It had served its purpose, to quickly spirit a helpless John Pilate from the Hog's Snout restaurant to the tall man's car, then to... wherever the hell this was. The bucket in the other corner was untouched. He looked at every inch of his prison, searching for a way out.

"Nothing," he said. "Just an empty steel box. I'm really in bad shape here."

Pilate got off his knees and stood up, shining the light at the walls again, checking out the door and the ledge by the access panel. Again, nothing. He hopped up to reach for the broken light bulb, managing to brush it with his fingertips. He stood underneath, shining the light on it, wondering if there might be a way to weaponize it. He traced the cord from the center of the room to the back where the cord disappeared into a hole.

"What the..." Pilate glimpsed a faded stencil spray painted on the wall just below the hole.

Xtra Keys Self Storage
5027 Suncrest Road
Key West, FL 33040

DO NOT STORE PERISHABLES
RENT DUE 5th of Month

"Oh my God," Pilate rasped. He was locked in a self-storage unit. "Clearly not climate controlled," he thought.

"Okay, you're a perishable. Still, this is good news," Simon said. *"You're not in an empty warehouse somewhere. Somebody is bound to show up and you can make noise and get out."*

"Yeah," Pilate said falling back on his haunches, then sitting on the floor. "Except this might be one of the storage businesses that got flooded out and closed in the hurricane last year. Some of them use old shipping containers as units. Sure smells like it."

"Well, that's depressing."

His mood plummeting, Pilate felt his energy going the same way. He lay on his back, the hard, hot floor adding to his misery.

A buzzing sound jarred him; his eyes opened.

"John?"

Another buzz.

"Johnny? Wake up."

His hand uncurled on the sheet, and the Tarkin figure, loosed from his grip, fell over the side of the bunk bed. He rolled off the Simon game, which went silent without his childhood weight pressing all the buttons at once.

"Daddy, where are you?" A little boy's voice broke the silence.

"Pete? Pete, honey?" Pilate said.

"You're never home," said a girl. It was Kara, his stepdaughter.

"I'm coming home kids, I promise," he said, inexplicably wet tears in the corners of his eyes.

Pilate awoke alone on the floor, clammy, cramping and miserable.

"Poor Kara. To lose one father is tragic, but to lose a second one, well that's just careless," Simon said. *"As for Peter, well... you aren't exactly around much, anyway."*

Pilate shook him off.

"I promise. I promise," be muttered. "I'll fix this."

The aura of heat before his eyes made every move an effort; his energy lower than the thirty percent left on his phone. The clock read 5:02 a.m. He went to his contacts, found Kate's number, and tapped the text messaging icon:

"Not sure you will get this but wanted you to know I spent these last hours thinking of you and the kids. Hard to explain--just can't always be present. Even when I'm in the next room. Sometimes takes all I have to be patient with anything. But I do love you all am so very sorry I made a mess of everything. No matter what happens if I survive I want to be a better person. Even if you don't love me anymore I want you to know I will always love you and Kara & Pete are everything to me."

He pressed send, and soon received the hateful error message in return. A thought struck his sluggish brain, and he went to one of the pencil-sized holes drilled in the front of the unit. He aimed the phone at the outside world, and tried to send the text again, only to receive another error message.

His head pounded like he had a massive hangover, a sunburn and an ice pick in his guts all at once. He sat back down and resolved to try again, swatting away a mosquito who had no problems getting inside the cage and biting him.

"Maybe you should try and reach somebody who can help you. You'll only panic Kate even if by some miracle that signal gets out," Simon cooed.

Pilate nodded, wiping sweat from his eyes and choking out a raspy, dry cough. He thumbed out a group message to Taters and Val.

"John Pilate. Locked in a unit I think at Xtra Keys Self Storage. Suncrest Road on Stock Island I think. Very hot in here. Not sure kidnapper will return. He has been gone for several hours. I need help. I am dying."

A loud clanking sound startled him. He looked up to see the access panel open an inch.

"Sir?"

Pilate had grown to hate that voice so much, but now he was ecstatic to hear it. He rose up on his elbow, summoning the strength to move closer to the access panel to feel the cool breeze.

"Sir?"

Pilate remained quiet.

"Sir? If you are awake, don't think I am foolish enough to open the big door. You need to tell me you're still with us."

Pilate sighed. "I'm too weak to do any harm, anyway." His throat protested with every word. "You have water?"

"Yes."

"Can I have some?"

"I think not." Honk, honk.

"Fuck you then," Pilate said, his words slurred with exhaustion.

"Sir, not nice. You know something, you are not a nice friend."

"I'm not your friend. How the hell do you know anything about me anyway?"

"I saw you at the bookstore. You signed my book and did not smile with grace and favor. You emailed and said we could be friends. And at the gym. I tried to be nice and give you a towel while you were talking to that woman who is not your wife. That's not nice."

Pilate searched his mind, fighting to remember if he had encountered anyone with a towel at the gym. "That woman is my trainer."

"You want to sweat with her?" his kidnapper said, honking.

"And you emailed and said to come meet you for a drink."

"What? I never did that." He sounded unsure.

"Well, it's obvious you did."

"Oh my god this guy is on fucking planet Mongo," Simon said.

Pilate gasped for a moment, trying to catch some cool air from the small gap. "Just tell me. What do you want?" Pilate's hand swept the ground seeking the large glass shard.

"I want you to be nice," he said. "I want you to not act so big. Be nice-nice to the little people."

"Jesus man, I *am* little people," Pilate rasped, his fingers finding and curling around the shard of glass. "Can I have some water, please?"

"I made you something."

"Can I please have some water? I can't handle another martini. On the wagon."

"No, this is morning. I made you coffee. Like you drink with your girlfriend at Frenchie's. Nice and hot. With cream and sugar. Here." The panel slid open all the way; the black nitrile-gloved hand slid a cup of coffee on a saucer on the ledge. "Come get it."

"No energy," Pilate said, slowly raising himself up.

"I think you will get the energy. It would not be nice-nice if you did not take this nice coffee."

Pilate efforted to his feet, a slight breeze from outside reviving him some. "How do I know you didn't poison it?"

The man honked. "Oh, that's silly. Why would I poison you, my friend? Not nice-nice."

"Yeah, and you can just leave me in here to rot, I suppose." He palmed the ruined martini glass.

"Drink the coffee sir," he said in monotone. "We can chat like nice friends over coffee."

Pilate staggered to the panel, one hand grasping the shard, the other his iPhone. He reached the ledge and peered out. It wasn't bright, there was no work light illuminating the hallway this time. He saw the outline of the tall, skinny man, with shoulder-length hair, slouching a foot or so from the panel.

"So you're a Jimmy Buffet fan? I like 'Fins.' What's your name, is it...Lovejoy? No--Strong?" Pilate said, pressing the screen on his phone at his side. The send button glimmered in the half-darkness, tempting him. He had to be sure. There would be only one chance.

"Oh, now you want to be friends. Just drink your coffee."

"Where's yours? It wouldn't be nice-nice to drink coffee in front of you," Pilate said. "Anyway you said we were friends having coffee--"

"I had mine," he said. "Now drink yours."

"Here's something for you, fucker." Pilate thrust his arm through the panel, the glass shard like the tip of a spear aimed at the lanky man. The man yelped, honked and parried; his thrust with the makeshift glass dagger had missed, not unlike Pilate's impotent punches at Val in the ring. Pilate shouted, cursing, his arm flailing helplessly at the man who had backed out of reach. The coffee cup fell inside his prison cell and shattered, hot liquid splattering his legs.

"Sir! Pull your arm back in now. Do it or I will have to hurt you." His monotone now that of a pimply high school junior, breaking comically with every other syllable.

"Fuck you," Pilate growled, his arm flailing like a dropped fire hose, whipping the air with menace. He realized he wasn't going to hit the guy, but every second of his bare arm in the relative cool of the hallway made his struggle worth it. Pilate pulled his arm back, keyed send and thrust his other arm out into the hallway, the iPhone mostly concealed in his fist.

The man pulled something from his pocket. He held it high where Pilate could see it. "I will tase you," he said, without the honking laughter.

"Come and try," Pilate said, his arm still exposed, though no longer flailing. Instead, he held it high, as if trying to play keep-away with a child.

"This is your last warning," the man said. "I mean it."

Pilate jerked his arm back inside, but kept the phone as close to the portal as he dared. "Alright, alright. Fine."

"Step away. Go to the back," the man ordered.

"Why? What are you going to do? Come in here and tase me, bro?" Pilate said, snickering bitterly but standing his ground. It was a standoff; the kidnapper couldn't tase him without coming close enough to risk being stabbed with the glass.

"Do it or I will forget to give you water."

"I don't have any water now," Pilate said.

"Step back and I will place a bottle of cool water on this ledge. After you imbibe that, we can discuss the future."

"How do I know you won't shut that panel and leave me here?"

"You don't. But that would not be nice."

"I have two children," Pilate said. "Please."

"Big man," his tormentor replied.

"Fuck off and die, you worthless piece of shit," Pilate said, sagging against the opening in the panel, filling his lungs.

"Move away, sir, or I will tase you in the face."

Pilate felt a fresh chill go through his body; his guts seized in a painful spasm. "I'm asking you one more time. Let me out. Please? Let me out. I miss my kids," Pilate said, his lungs reviving with each gasp of the cooler air.

Pilate felt the phone vibrate. He read the message notification:

"WE ARE ON THE WAY. DON'T LOSE HOPE. MODELOS CHILLING. STAY STRONG. – TM"

"I will count to three," the man said. "One."

"The cops will be the least of your worries if I die in here, you know."

"Two."

"Taters may be a little low right now, but he's pretty mean when somebody messes with his friends. And Kate? Ever hear about her aim with a shotgun?"

"Three."

Pilate jerked away from the panel, but before the kidnapper could slam it shut a new sound came faintly in the distance – the wail of police sirens.

"Do you hear that, asshole? That's the cops. They know where I am. You left me my cell phone, you…you amateur!"

The panel slammed shut and the kidnapper's voice came one last time, cold and angry but somehow not entirely disappointed. ""I am sorry you could not be nice." Pilate heard the man's footfalls receding rapidly as he ran down the hallway. The sirens grew louder but were still far away.

"Have a nice-nice day, you creepy fucking nutjob," Pilate whispered, falling to his knees, his eyes greedily reading and rereading the message from Taters.

The sirens were louder still as he slipped further down to the floor, laying on his side, looking at the photo of Peter and Kara.

"Hold on, Johnny. Hold on," Simon said.

"I'm good," he rasped. "I'm coming home, kids. Gonna fix it."

"Stay awake," Simon said. *"They need to be able to find you fast. Bang on the door."*

"Okay. But you have to go now, Simon," Pilate whispered.

"Not until you're alright, Johnny. Not until then."

THE END

AFTERWORD

Ten years. That's a lot of days, minutes, and seconds.

Seven installments of the John Pilate Mysteries. That's a lot of pages and words.

So, you may be wondering why *Pilate's Shadow* is a very long story rather than a full-blown novel? I don't know; when I sat down to write, this was the result. I didn't want to force anything or pad the story to get to a certain length. I just wanted to tell a good tale and get John Pilate back on the hot seat. Achieving this in 14,000 words or so is how it shook out.

Finishing *Pilate's Shadow* during this tenth anniversary year of the first book's publication had me looking back to the days when I first moved to Kansas City to take a new job and be with my soon-to-be wife, leaving behind a tiny town in southeast Nebraska with a dark chapter in its history.

Pilate's Cross was meant to be a one-off book, based loosely on a true story from that town, a tragic murder-suicide at a tiny land-grant college in 1950. Soon after the book came out, I realized *Pilate's Cross* was more than just a "one-off"; it was a new world of fun characters navigating interesting situations with myriad possibilities. Indeed, the best was yet to come.

In *Pilate's Cross*, John Pilate arrived in Cross Township broken and barely hanging on. The ensuing novels followed his ups and downs, his friends and foes, exotic travels, and most importantly, his battles with his inner demon, Simon. As we arrived at *Pilate's Rose*, a battered Pilate has started to confront the reasons why he does the things he does. In *Pilate's Shadow*, he's in full-blown panic mode as psychotherapy and life events force him to honestly confront the origins of his pain. Of course, he also has a bad guy showing up to complicate things.

In this life, some are luckier than others, but nobody gets out unscathed. Mental health issues touch us all, whether it be a relative, a friend, or ourselves. It can be genetic in origin, or perhaps the lingering hangover for a hideous cocktail of abuse, neglect, and cruelty.

Pilate has certainly had his share of bad stuff, and he's coming to terms with the fact that he doesn't need antidepressants simply because he was "broken" at birth. No, he experienced childhood trauma that festered into adulthood. This has a multiplier effect on Pilate, as his decision-making, relationships, and his very sanity is hampered by depression, low self-esteem, and crippling anxiety attacks.

There lies the thesis of the John Pilate Mysteries: our fractured, all-too-human hero trying to outwit the bad guys and live another day.

As we move forward to the next ten years, we'll see if Pilate can confront his dark side, and learn to live with it in a way that is not ultimately self-destructive. I'm guessing we all do that in our own ways. I know I do.

I'm often asked if John Pilate is me.

Well, yeah. Of course, he is.

But he's you, too. And so is Kate, and Taters, and the rest of the gang. Just remember, though, they are fictional, and a lot of the stuff that happens in these books is not necessarily inspired by real life. Much of it is just that spice in the stew, that hint of Lillet in a fine Vesper martini.

So, here's to ten years.

Thanks so much for sticking with John. You know, I wanted to quit after the third book, but couldn't seem to seal the deal. John kept calling. (Or was it Simon?)

That said, there's a new novel on the way, and this little story I tucked into a special edition of *Pilate's Rose* is, in many ways, the introduction. I see it as the bridge between the first six parts of the series and what looks to be the last six, which will be coming your way over the next few years.

I'm very curious to see how it all ends up. Until next time…keep reading.

J. Alexander Greenwood
Kansas City, Mo
2019

P.S. Special thanks to my cover artist, Jason McIntyre, and my editor, Robert Hayes, Jr. Literally couldn't do it without them.

***

Like this series? Your positive reviews encourage me to write more books and helps new readers find me. It only takes a minute, and you'll love yourself in the morning.
Please leave a starred review on Amazon.com right now.
***